CW00473089

# FINDING

# CHARLIE

# A NOVEL BY MEGAN GANT

Megan Gant

# CHAPTER ONE

I was never one to interfere. When I was 15, I overheard at a family party that my paternal Grandfather had been paying my Mother on a monthly basis to keep her from divorcing my father. I couldn't ask why so I just kept it to myself. Just like the time, three years later, when I found out that the same money my Grandfather was paying my Mother she was then using to fund my aunt's bi-monthly stay at the local rehab centre. Safe to say my 18<sup>th</sup>

birthday didn't go as expected. I'd always

known there was something going on. I'm

constantly underestimated by my Mother. There

is always something being covered up by my

family but I never expected the biggest cover up

of all to be my brother's death.


Charlie died when he was 16, a terrible

drowning accident in the family pool one

summer holiday. Our family is wealthy and our

Hamptons home is the classic millionaire's

holiday home. The décor is white and airy, with

dark wooden floors. There are large French

doors leading out to the crisp green grass

overlooking our own private jetty onto the

waterfront and still standing is the 30 year old wooden play frame we used to play on. The perfect image of the perfect family.

Being just 3 and a half years old when my brother died, I've only ever known that every time the 18th of August rolls around my family dresses in their Sunday best and throws an event with their friends along with half the reporters from the Upper East Side. It would be a memorial, but no one was ever sad enough nor do people even mention the boy that died. We always had a picture of Charlie that, initially, was a 4ft poster surrounded by flowers and candles. The size of it started to diminish over the years and last year was no different. The only thing that determined this event was anything like a memorial was the photo of Charlie on the mantlepiece where it had sat for the past 20 years. I was the only person to place a flower beside him.

The big day started just like any other day. The breakfast table was filled with plates of fresh fruit from the farmers market, freshly baked crepes and croissants. Too much food for three people to pick at for 10 minutes before someone gets bored with the suffocating silence filling the dining room.

I joined my parents, my Mother and Father sitting at either end of the table with me in the middle. That's got to be a metaphor for something. I could sense my Mother's gaze on me while she sipped her tea. Every move I made was seen, it's something I've gotten used to over the years. My Father, however, couldn't care less.

William Simmonds Jr is the owner of one of New York's largest business empires. Inherited from his Father when he took an early retirement, my Father had been running Simmonds and Son Industries since he was 30 years old. He never wanted the responsibility of such a large company. If he had his way, he'd be living in the country with 2 kids, a dog and a partner who loved him. Dad is very laid back. As long as I'm safe and happy then that's all that matters.

'Are you coming to the event this evening Katheryn?' My Mother's voice breaks the silence in the room.

'Event? You mean Charlie's memorial?' I'm the one to call out the bullshit, no matter how much it riles up my Mother. Her demeaner automatically changes, she's defensive and snappy.

'Yes, Charlie's memorial – are you going to show your face? I have managed to get a piece in Vanity Fair to cover the 20th anniversary of his tragic passing.' This must be a joke. Was this another business venture for her?

'What? You're monetising your own son's death? Wow, I always knew these events weren't really to remember Charlie but at least before you would hide the fact you were making money off of his death. Until now.'

'Katheryn do you really have to be so dramatic? All I'm doing is a simple interview and they asked for a family picture and we're going to do it. We have to at least show that the Simmonds' family are stronger than ever, if not for us, at least for the business.' I couldn't believe what I was hearing, surely my Father must have an opinion on this?

'Dad, are you ok with this. Do you hear what she's saying?' The urgency in my voice comes across as anger. My Father looks up over his paper briefly.

'It's what your Mother wants.'

'That's not what I asked Dad. Do you really think this is a good idea?'

He stares at me while darting back to my Mother, as if he was checking if she was looking. He leans over and holds my hand.

'It's one article Kate, it's what your Mother wants.' He squeezed my hand before I pulled away. Could he not stand up for what's right? Was he too scared? I couldn't take this. I stood, throwing my napkin on the table before turning to my Mother.

'It's not just one article though is it? It's one of the other twenty she'd had done. You're unbelievable.' I left the dining room, grabbing my bag on the way out of the apartment, letting my parents sit in the silence they love so much.


As soon as I got access to my trust fund at 18 I bought my first apartment in Brooklyn. Secret apartment that is. There was no way my Mother could ever find out about this. If she knew a Simmonds girl was living in Brooklyn god help us all. I had to get out of the family home at least for a couple of days where I could say I was staying with friends. Ever since I found out my Grandfather was paying my Mother to keep quiet about my Father's affair just so the scandal wouldn't affect business, it was like someone opened my eyes for me.

Everything I could remember from my

childhood became a little clearer, how my

Father could never have a say on anything and

that all that my Mother had ever done was

because she was getting paid for it. There's no

love there, it's just power. Monetary power. A

perfect marriage on the Upper East Side.

I didn't remember the day my brother

died, yet it still haunts me. I regretted asking my

Mother about him. She was never kind with her

words. Charlie was the golden boy, the

favourite. He was the heir to the family business

and with him gone, it was just me, which didn't

look good in the opinion of my family. A

woman taking over a business, how truly terrifying.

My suspicions started on the night of the 5<sup>th</sup> anniversary of his death. I was 9 years old. I remember wearing a baby pink coloured shift dress with the hem made longer, specifically requested by my Mother, and all night long all I did was sit and watch. My Mother used to tell me I scared people away because all I would do at events she would host was sit and watch the people around me. But what I did notice was that not one person was sad my brother was dead and had been gone for 5 years. My Mother would be mingling with the guests who were dressed just as glamorously as she was, talking about the latest trends in fashion or what was said at the last Mothers' meeting they had.

Nothing was ever about Charlie and that's what

I couldn't understand. How can a family go

from worshiping their son to acting like he

never existed? The apartment was where I

started keeping my evidence. Notebooks of

things I've heard in passing, things I've pieced

together myself. But it's never came to fruition.

I didn't know what I was trying to prove at this

point. Was I trying to prove my Mother is

heartless? Or was it the fact my Father was now

just as bad and I could not face that? Either

way, something was not right.

I spent most of my day dreading this

evening before I had to get ready. The 20th year

of pretending we're a family surviving without

Charlie was now to be commemorated with a photo in Vanity Fair that might as well be labelled *Frauds*. Mother summoned me back to the house an hour earlier so she could supervise me getting ready, this simply consisted of her looking at the 2 black dresses I chose and tutting at both of them.

'Couldn't you have chosen something happier?' I rolled my eyes as I turned to face her.

'Sorry but some of us are sad their brother has been dead for 20 years. Forgive me Mother for having a heart.' There was no emotion in her face, just disgust.

'You'll never get married with a mouth like that.'

'Who says I want to get married.' Here we go, back onto pawning me off. Prepare for the guilt trip in 3, 2, 1.

'Katheryn! Must you really do this today, after everything I've done for you tonight.' You've got to be kidding me.

'Everything you've done for *me*? This isn't for me. This isn't even meant to be for you or Dad. This is for Charlie remember? Why do you act like he never existed but manage to use his death as your social event of the year? What is wrong with you?' I can't cope with being in the same room as her. I zip my dress up, leave the room and head for the living room with not one hesitation from her to try to stop me.

The living room was decked out with fresh bouquets of flowers, trays of champagne, and just a hint of deceit in the air. My Father walked down the stairs in a new suit but didn't walk past me.

'I'm sorry Kate. For this morning. I agree with you. I don't want to do this, I never have. From day one this has all been a social construct created by your Mother.'
My Father did this sometimes. When Eleanor wasn't in ear shot, we had these moments, precious moments where he talked to me, genuinely and whole heartedly. I savoured them but I also hated them. What kind of marriage consists of that?

'Dad, it's okay. I know. Let's just get through this and then we never have to think about it again.' I felt a constant need to reassure him. An overwhelming need to make sure he didn't do anything silly. He gave me a kiss on the cheek and walked towards the room where my Mother was getting ready.

Living in a penthouse was all well and good until you realised anyone could get into the elevator and walk into your home. Within moments in walked my Grandfather.

Grandfather Simmonds still treated me like a little girl. He also had an extremely Victorian mindset when it comes to women. Women should never get their hands dirty with business, they are only here to serve their men. That kind of bullshit.

'Papa! How good to see you!' I must get the talent of putting on a face from my Mother.

'Katy! Katy! Haven't you grown into a lovely woman!' Oh, did I also mention very inappropriate towards women too, whether you're related or not. His hands linger on my waist a little too long before I move away, directing him into the main room.

'A drink? Let me get you some champagne - I'll let Mum know you're here.' I walked as quick as I could in 6 inch heels on marble flooring towards the room where my Mother was getting ready. I swiftly opened the door and let my parents know my Grandfather had arrived. The tension in that room was suffocating . I stepped away but it seemed whatever was said or done in that room was seeping out into the whole house.

Within 20 minutes our whole apartment was filled with the best of the best from the Upper East Side. I didn't know one person bar my family but the plus side of being part of a rich family in New York is that everyone knows you or at least they think they do. I had to hold conversations with news reporters who were simply there to know about the upcoming business partnership my Father was creating and  fashion reporters who wanted to know who

I was wearing and if I'd be attending fashion week this year. I lied to them all. Sorry Mother.

It was about 3 hours in and the last of the guests were leaving. Until that point I realised no one had made a speech. I wasn't expecting one for Charlie but I was at least expecting one from my Mother, just out of courtesy. It's not like her at all to not address her guests. I looked around and she wasn't in the main room. I made my way down the hall and saw my Mother and Grandfather whispering in the spare room. I hid behind the wall and listened.

'I can't keep doing this anymore. I cannot. It's too much.'

'Eleanor, you need to calm down, nothing good will come from you having a breakdown.' I had never heard my Mother talk like this, let alone to my Grandfather.

'We've been lying for 20 years Billy. Something needs to change. It's not going to stay secret forever.'

'Only us 3 know Charlie isn't dead. Nothing is going to get out. We paid the boy to keep his mouth shut. It's not going to get out.' It was at that moment I felt my heart sink to my stomach. I found myself subconsciously slipping my shoes off, turning around and heading for the exit. It was like all my senses had stopped, I couldn't hear anything but my heart beating in my chest.

# CHAPTER TWO

Somehow I ended back at my apartment. I
closed the front door and leaned against it until I
found myself sitting on the floor. For 20 years I
was told my brother had tragically died,
drowning in the swimming pool. The very
swimming pool I couldn't bear dipping my toes
into for the whole summer after they told me
how he died. The brother I never got the chance

to know had been alive this whole time. I felt betrayed. Why would my family lie to me about this?

After a few hours I dragged myself into bed just to stare at the ceiling. The blood in my body started to feel restless, not yet boiling but simmering on the surface. I couldn't sit still. I got up and reached under my bed, pulling out a large clear storage box containing all the notebooks I'd kept since I was 9 years old. My diaries throughout adolescence, scrapbooks with paper clippings about my family and Charlie's death. Maybe some of this could be useful in finding my brother. I started going through them. Turning each page and seeing his face. I couldn't help but feel guilty. Guilty for being a part of this family, guilty for not finding this out sooner, but what was I meant to do? What could I do now?

I haven't returned home in 2 days and not one phone call from my parents. My apartment now looks like a scene from a detective movie. I've pinned pictures and clippings on the walls. I have a whiteboard with a timeline of everything I've recorded, every business deal since Charlie's disappearance, every tiny detail I could find but with all honesty it's not going to get me far. I need to do more. As I was working on my wall of evidence (that sounds badass right?), a knock startled me. I try to cover the wall up but with no luck. The knocking was loud and persistent so I rush over to open the door. A big mistake. I open the door to my Grandfather standing there in an expensive black pinstripe suit holding a black leather suitcase – how very 1920's.

'So this is where you've been hiding.' His gravelly voice made me shudder. I tried to lean my weight onto the door to stop him from coming in but he pushed his way in.

'Papa, what are you doing here? How did you know I was here?' He walked straight in towards The Wall of Evidence, ignoring me completely. He observed everything in front of him until he turned around, staring blankly at me.

'I had you followed.'

'You had me followed?' I was shocked but not exactly surprised.

'I know you heard something from the other night. I saw you running out of the apartment, shoes in hand. It was all very dramatic Katy.' He'd shuffled closer to me, we were standing face to face, close enough for me to know all he's had that morning was a large black coffee for breakfast. Tread carefully Katheryn.

'Fine. You're right. I heard. Charlie is still alive. But I'm not going to out this secret to anyone.'

'Oh really? You're not going to tell a soul? Because it looks as if you've been doing quite a bit of work over there trying to figure this all out.' He swung his arm back over towards The Wall, proving his point. I sighed.

'Papa, I just want to know where my brother is. You know Mum will never tell me. Can't you just help me?' He scoffed at my plea for help.

'Katheryn. You need to let this go.'

'No – why did you pay him off to leave the family? What could a 16 year old do to make you do that?'

'That's none of your business. What happened, happened. You don't need to be digging up old dirt, just let it be.' That wasn't convincing at all. Something was telling me this was just the tip of the iceberg.

'Papa, I'm not going to let it be. My brother is out there and has been for 20 years. I will do this on my own if I have to.' His demeaner changed. His shoulders dropped and he leant in to whisper into my ear.

'That's all I wanted you to say.' I backed away from his wispy breath on my skin, I stare at him with confusion, he just smiled at me.

'I will give you the contact details of a private investigator but in return you must give up your place in the family. No more trust fund. No more access to *my* money. No more contact.' I took a large breath and stepped back.

'Fine.'

He scoffed again as he walks towards the front door.

'You won't like what you find Katheryn. I'll send you the details you need, you will be cut off within 24 hours.' He turned and leant in for a kiss on the cheek, 'You were always such a good girl. Whatever happened?' With a squeeze of my arm, he left my apartment. I double locked the door as soon as he was gone and fell into the sofa. It felt like the wind had been taken out of my chest. I couldn't care less about the money, I just didn't understand why it was needed for me to be cut out of the family. Did the same happen to Charlie? Did he know something that he shouldn't have?

I had 24 hours before I was cut off. I needed a plan of action. I immediately started pulling everything down from my walls and stuffing it into plastic folders, making sure I wasn't forgetting anything important. I fetched my old brown leather gym bag from under my bed, grabbing the first items of clothing to hand and throwing them into the bag alongside the plastic folders and my passport. Next thing I needed was money. If I was going to be cut off then my bank cards won't work, I needed cash. I cleared up my apartment as best as I could in such little time. All personal photos were packed into boxes in the locked spare room, leaving little to no trace of me in this apartment.

I made it into the city and made a beeline to the bank. I tried to make myself look as calm as possible. The slouchy blue mom jeans were on, paired with a black and white striped top along with my trusty Converse and a grey knitted cardigan, perhaps not the best outfit to wear on the Upper East Side when trying to withdraw thousands of pounds but I'm going for practicality if I'm essentially going on the run to find a missing person. Thankfully there was no queue and I was seen to immediately.

'Ah Miss Simmonds, haven't seen you for a while, what can I do for you?' Sebastian Delaney was the manager of this branch and also my boyfriend, secret boyfriend of course.

Every time I came into the bank he greeted me as if he didn't know me.

'Hi, I need to withdraw some money, preferably all of it...' His eyebrows raised, looking at me with suspicion. I handed over my details not letting one hint of emotion pass through the Perspex dividing us. He processed my details and looked back up at me.

'You have too much money in your account. We cannot withdraw that amount to you in cash. Certainly not just over the counter.'

'Well, how much do I have? It can't be that much, I hardly ever touch it, not since I bought my apartment.' I become agitated, even though this had only been a couple of minutes I felt like time was ticking on.

'You have in the region of $2.3 million left. It's gained a hefty amount of interest since you were 18.' Shit. That was a lot of money.

'Right. Ok. How much can I take out today?' Sebastian noticed my body language, he could tell I was getting frustrated.

'You can take $20,000. But in my office.' This better not take long.

'Ok fine.' I walk to the end of the corridor and meet Sebastian. He started acting paranoid, as if someone was following him as we made our way to his office. He opened the door and I followed, taking a seat at his desk. He sat opposite and leant back.

'Are you going to tell me what's going on?' His whole tone changed and he was no longer talking to me as his customer. His stare was piercing. He did this a lot. Maybe time for a little back story.

I've always had a crush on Sebastian but the only thing was, he's 13 years older than me. I always booked my bank meetings in with him but around 3 years ago I once again had an argument with my Mother and I ended up getting drunk at the closest bar when Sebastian was just so conveniently there too. He gave me that stare then which happens to be a weakness of mine. I ended up telling him about my Father's affair and how my Grandfather was paying my Mother to keep quiet (I politely refrained from mentioning the dirty money details). The night ended with him taking me back to Brooklyn. He didn't leave my side and didn't judge me on any of the information I told him nor how drunk I was. He's a good person, and very protective of me. He's also a great kisser. Since then, we've been seeing each other. In secret, of course.

'Well..?' His thick New York accent brings me back into the room.

'Seb, it's complicated. I just need to withdraw some money.' He immediately gets up and walks to the door locking it before sitting back down into his chair leaning over his desk.

'Are you in trouble Kate?' I only really liked it when he called me Kate.

'No, at least not yet. My Grandfather's cut me off and I need to leave town for a little while.' His stare didn't let up until I mumbled a quiet 'please'.

'I can get you $20,000 in cash today. Will that be enough?'

'That's enough, thank you.' I had pulled the sleeves of my cardigan down over my hands, a common coping mechanism whenever I became anxious. Sebastian left the office to go down into the vault, locking the door on the way out.

It was a silent 2 minutes until my phone vibrated. An email notification from my Grandfather.

*To: Katheryn Simmonds*

*From: William Simmonds Snr*

*Subject: Confidential Information*

*Katheryn.*

*As per our agreement. See attachment.*

*Regards,*

*Billy.*

--------

Short and sweet. I opened the attachment and there it was, as promised, the name and phone number for a Mr Eric Fernsby. I saved the number in my phone and called him. It rang 3 times until he picked up.

'Hi, is that Mr Fernsby?' I tried to make myself sound like I knew what I was doing, I'm not sure how well that came across.

'Speaking. How can I help?' His voice was strong and clear, quite the opposite to mine.

'My name is Katheryn, Billy Simmonds' Granddaughter. He gave me your number as I'd like your help in looking for my brother?' I was fully aware that seeing as this contact came from my Grandfather that this could involve foul play but at this point I'm not afraid of that.

'Yes, he's mentioned you'd be calling me. I've already started digging. I've got a potential lead in the Nevada area. Can I email you the details?'

'Oh. Wow, ok. Of course, please.' Eric hung up immediately. Remind me to teach him some telephone manners. I slipped my phone back into my bag as Sebastian walked back into the room.

He was carrying the cash in a white plastic bag. He sat down, unzipped the bag and started counting the rolls of cash in front of me. Once he finished he rolled the cash back up and placed the rolls back into the plastic bag, pushing it across the desk towards me.

'Where are you going?'

'Nevada, for now. I'll call you once I get there.'

'Are you going to be ok?' He was giving me that look again.

'Of course. It's me, I'm always ok.' That was meant to come out more reassuring than it did.

'I've been thinking. Whatever you're doing, if you need extra money, just ask me. I'll transfer the rest of your money into a new account that only I have access to, just call me and I will get the money to you.'

'Sebastian, you could lose your job if anyone found out. Plus there'd be no way I could get the money, I think I'm going to be moving about a lot.'

'Then take a spare emergency debit card. It'll be in my name so no one would suspect you. I know what your family are like.'

'Sebastian, I can't.'

'You can. I'll order a card to be made and we'll work out a way to get it to you. Please Kate. Let me help you.' Told you he was a good guy.

'Alright fine. But if you get fired –'

' – then that's on me.' I smiled at him and reached for the money. I stuff it in my bag before zipping it up and standing, placing the bag on my shoulder. Sebastian comes walking round to face me.

'Thank you Sebastian. For everything.'

I lean in and kiss him on the cheek before turning out the door until he grabs my arm and pulls me in for one hell of a goodbye kiss.

He eventually pulls away

'Be safe.'

'I will.'

With that I walked out of the room, not looking back. I made my way through the main lobby and on to the street. As I started walking, I felt a wave of uncertainty washing over me. Was I doing the right thing? Maybe Charlie didn't want to be found? I couldn't help but think I could maybe find something back at my parent's house. There was never a good time to go hunting through their stuff to find the

evidence I needed. Until now.

# CHAPTER THREE

As I walk up Lexington Ave, I see my parents getting out of a car and heading into Bloomingdales. This gives me the perfect opportunity to head home before I have to leave. I call a taxi and head to the house.

As soon as I sit down in the cab, my phone vibrates with another email notification, this time from Eric.

*To: Katheryn Simmonds*

*From: E.Fernsby*

*Subject: C.Simmonds*

*Miss Simmonds.*

*As discussed earlier I have managed to track a viable lead in Las Vegas connected to your brother. However, I would normally fly out with you but on this occasion I'm unable to, though I have arranged for my son to meet you out there. He is part of the family business so you don't need to worry. Everything is still fully confidential.*

*Book yourself onto the next flight and he'll meet you at McCarren Airport. I've passed your number on to him.*

*Speak soon.*

*E.Fernsby*

--

Vegas, of all places? The taxi pulled up outside the apartment block. I shoved my phone back into my bag and headed into the lobby. I could not process that email right now. I tried to keep a low profile as I went into the lift pressed the button to lift me up into the house that was no longer my home. The doors opened and I turned the corner, making sure no one was home. I swiftly made my way down the corridor and into my parent's bedroom, closing the door behind me. I turned to my left into my Mother's walk in closet, heading straight for the rail of designer gowns. Pushing them apart I found the safe located in the middle of the wall. The safe was forbidden. Not even my Father had access to this, so there's got to be something in there that doesn't want to be found. My Mother was a lot of things: manipulative; conniving; secretive; a liar, but she wasn't overtly clever when it comes to passwords. One touch of the keypad with the digits of her birthday and I was in. Did she know nothing about password security?

Inside the imbedded steel box were leather folders, each one with a family member's name on, including one for me and one for Charlie. I grabbed both of them and put them in my bag. Riffling through the safe I came across a gun. A small gun, black and loaded. It's not unusual to have a gun but why was it loaded and why was it locked in my Mother's safe? What was she afraid of? *Who* was she afraid of? I'd never fired a gun, ever. I don't believe in them. I don't believe we should have access to them. I toyed with my principles staring at this gun in my hand, feeling the smooth metal with my fingertips. I found myself unloading the gun. The bullets fell carelessly into my bag eventually along with the gun. I didn't overthink it, instead I tried to rationalise it. It was better if I had the gun, it was better with me than here. If it was here, someone could use it. If it was with me, I knew it wouldn't get used. Right? I closed the safe door making sure the dresses were back where they were, covering any trace of me being there.

I made a swift exit back onto the busy New York street walking with no destination. I felt as if everything that had happened the last 12 hours was starting to crash around me and weigh on my chest. I stumbled into a cobbled alley way to try and catch my breath. I pulled the bag off of my shoulder and dropped to the floor beside it, my chest feeling like I had a hundred bricks on top of me, my throat closing with every breath I took. I closed my eyes to try and stop the tears falling without warning, to try and focus on my breathing, and then my hands went numb. Panic attacks started making an appearance in my life when I was around 15, the same time I found out the first big secret from my family. Initially they were somewhat brief but overtime they have evolved. They completely incapacitate me. My limbs went numb, I could not breathe, I could not move.

# CHAPTER FOUR

There's something comforting about anxiety. At least for me. I perhaps it's the only consistent thing I've become accustomed to, and it's mine and only mine. I've always felt like an outsider to my family, that's the root of it all. I've never liked the fancy parties or the expensive clothes. It all seems so overwhelming to me and nothing was ever done without the need of wanting to be the best, or look the best. In the long term, it's all just a waste of time.

I picked myself back up from off the floor. My breathing had calmed and with my brain regaining consciousness I jumped in a taxi taking me to the airport. I booked the next flight to Vegas on my phone and I couldn't tell if it was the lasting effects of the panic attack or not but I as calm. It was an eerie calm. Everything was silent. This 'adventure', albeit just beginning, was becoming a little more taxing than I thought it would be. I was beginning to wonder if this was really worth it.

Within 5 hours I touched down at McCarren airport. I checked the time on my phone. It was coming up to 7pm, somehow it felt later. The exhaustion from the last few days with the added few hours of jet lag had really grabbed a hold of me. I made my way through the airport bypassing baggage claim and straight into arrivals, and there was a man standing there with piece of paper stating my name.

Harvey Fernsby. He stood in the middle of an airport, the only person wearing a tailored Armani three piece suit, clearly uncomfortable to be even standing in such a communal space that didn't have once ounce of gold leaf detailing. Not that I'm judgemental, though for first impressions I think I'm pretty spot on.

'Miss Simmonds?' His voice was deep, smooth not gravelly but there was something about it that made me instantly take a deep breath as if to armour myself. I walked closer and shook his hand, not breaking eye contact.

'Hi, sorry, I didn't catch your name...' He lets go of my hand, folds up the paper with my name on it, pushes it within his fancy suit, in turn pulling out a business card and handing it over.

'Harvey. Harvey Fernsby' He smirks at me and places his hand on the bottom of my back. 'Shall we head to the hotel?' Without me accepting, we're already moving towards the exit of the airport.

It's a half an hour drive to the hotel. Harvey of course had a driver to escort us. Sitting in the back of the car, I felt my eyes getting heavier. I leant my head against the window and moved my bag of possessions to my lap, holding them tight against my body. I felt a presence getting closer to me but I as almost too tired to care. I tried to get a little bit of shut eye before the hard work had to start. My mind started to drift off, my body started to get comfortable with the idea of a little rest until the presence I felt started to move onto me.

I felt Harvey place his hand on my knee. I kept my eyes closed, I didn't move a muscle. I felt his body shift turning towards me, his head almost resting on my shoulder. His hand started to graze further up my leg as he whispered in my ear telling me to not worry. I wanted to cry.

Harvey's hand got to the top of my leg and I had no idea what to do. He squeezed my thigh, once. Twice. Then dug his nails into my leg, which instantly made me jump. My eyes opened instantly and his face was right in front of me. That same smirk laced all over. He didn't move. I felt like I couldn't breathe.

'I didn't mean to wake you sweetheart.' His hand began to retract but still managed to trace over my jeans.

'What the fuck are you doing?' I tried to pull away but I was as far away as I could be in the back of the car. He still didn't move away from me.

'I was just making sure you were relaxed.'

'No. You were assaulting me. Get the fuck off me.' I pushed him away but he just came back, this time holding my shoulders down against the inside of the car door, his body completely covering me, his eyes frantically moving across my face.

'How dare you. You really are ungrateful. Your Grandfather has given you the opportunity to find your brother and then you do this? You accuse me of assaulting you? You need to learn to watch your mouth sweetheart.' He jolted my body further into the car door before he moved back to his side of the car. I slowly pulled myself up back into the seat. The car was filled with silence up until we arrive at the hotel and even then it was only the sound of car doors opening and closing that filled the space.

Harvey was already in the hotel lobby as I made my way through the glass doors. The hotel was monochrome with marble flooring, glass and mirrors cover every inch of wall and the most extravagant light fitting I had ever seen hung into the centre of the room. I walked further into the lobby towards Harvey, who was in deep conversation with a member of the hotel staff. As I got closer to him, he excused himself with a smile and sauntered over to me, ensuring distance was created between me and the member of staff. His face dropped as I opened my mouth.

'Where do I check in?' I said quickly and quietly, almost avoiding eye contact. Reaching into his jacket, he pulled out a room key card.

'Just go straight up. Room 244.' Hesitantly, I took the room key and muttered a small thank you before heading towards the elevator. My legs just about got me to the elevator. As the doors closed, my back sunk into the wall and I instantly let out a deep sigh. I as exhausted. I dug around in my bag looking for my phone. Two new messages. From Sebastian.

*Hey, just to let you know, I've sorted the money out. Let me know where you are and I'll get some money to you. S x*

*I'm starting to worry, you should have landed by now. Text me when you get to the hotel. S x*

I walked out of the elevator and immediately replied.

*Seb, I'm so sorry I've only just checked my phone. I'm at the hotel now. I'll send you the details asap, I need a nap – this is more exhausting than I thought. Xx*

I dumped my phone back in my bag and made my way into the corridor.

Room 244 was right at the end of the longest corridor. The door was different to all the others in the hotel. It was larger and a dark oak, even the numbers nailed to the door were gold instead of the standard metallic silver. It screamed Harvey Fernsby. Pushing the door open, I walked into a large open space with two archways either side leading to bedrooms, everything decorated just like the lobby, pretentious. The open space was graced with two sofas facing each other, a coffee table in between and a drinks trolly at the end. What more should be expected from Harvey?

I walked into the bedroom on the right-hand side, the least of the two that looks like Harvey's. I placed my bag down by the bed, grabbing some spare clothes that I packed and go straight into the en-suite to run a bath. I sat on the side and closed my eyes, trying to get my head around everything that happened in the car. I could still feel his hands all over me, like they had left an indent in my skin. A loud thumping knock at the door jolted me out of my thoughts. I quickly turned the tap off and open the door.

'Turndown Service?' A young man in hotel uniform smiles at me.

'Um, sure. Just this room though please. I'm going to jump in the bath, so you can let yourself out when you're done.' I opened the door further, leaving him to follow me into my bedroom. I grabbed the towels off of the side table and headed into the en-suite, locking the door behind me.

# CHAPTER FIVE

The hot water on my skin helps me to feel like

I'm getting Harvey's fingerprints off of me. I

sink down deeper into the bath, letting my head

go fully under, the water covering my face.

I never used to like having baths. I was 15 when

I discovered how much they helped. When

things became a bit too much at home or if it

was Charlie's birthday and my Mother would

put on another face for her friends proclaiming

how much she missed him, I would always leave to go run a bath. Nothing special. I would just sit and stare at the wall until I submerged myself into the water to see how long I could hold my breath. I never lasted that long.

I changed into a pair of denim shorts I bought with me and an old grey jumper I bought for comfort. I didn't think to bring pyjamas. I stepped out of the en-suite, scrunching my wet hair into a towel to see my bed as still perfectly made. Perhaps turndown services were different in Nevada? I looked into the living area and saw Harvey sitting on the sofa facing my room with a whiskey in his hand. I dropped the towel on the bed and walked towards the sofa closest to me.

'Hey, didn't see you there.' His eyes didn't leave my body, though this time there was something behind them. His eyes eventually met mine.

'Fancy a drink?' He gestured to the whiskey in his hand.

'Go on then.' I gave in and walk round to sit on the sofa. Harvey had his back to me whilst he poured the drink. I got comfortable on the sofa as he turned back round to hand me my drink.

'Here.' Harvey handed me my drink. 'Nice bath?'

I took a sip of my drink, wincing slightly as the whisky went down.

'It was alright thanks. Though, one of the hotel staff came by to do a turndown service and they haven't touched my bed…unless a turndown service is different around here?' Harvey scoffs at my sarcasm though replies with his own.

'That's not good at all, is it? How's your drink?' He used his own drink to gesture towards mine.

'Nice actually.' I took another sip. 'What's the plan for tomorrow Harvey?' He inhales deeply.

'We will be staying here.' I looked up from my drink.

'What? I thought your Dad said we had a lead?'

Harvey shifted slightly in his seat.

'We do, but something else has come up that I need to take care of. We're going to stay here until the lead we have changes then we will make moves.'

'Sorry – you're telling me that I've flown to Nevada and we're not even going to be doing anything to find my brother? That's the whole reason I came here Harvey! Not to sit around waiting for you to finish whatever job you have to do.' I stand up but I'm dizzy. The whole room felt like it was spinning until I felt Harvey's hands holding my arms, telling me to sit back down.

'Looks like you've stood up too quickly. Here.' He pressed the glass of whiskey into my hand making sure I grab hold of it. 'Just take a minute.'

Harvey stayed standing in front of me, eventually crouching down, his hands back on my thighs and his eyes fixed on mine.

'Sorry I—I don't understand. Maybe I need to go to bed.' I exhaled. What felt like a thousand heavy weights lift off of my chest yet the room was still moving around me. I tried to centre myself but the only point of focus as Harvey.

'Kate, I need you to focus now.' Harvey's hands were heavy on my thighs once more. 'Who's Sebastian?'

I immediately stopped breathing. Everything became a little clearer. Harvey had spiked my drink to get information out of me.

'How do you know about Sebastian?' I felt the panic surge through me. Harvey moved closer towards me, his face almost touching mine.

'Who is Sebastian?' With each word he spoke, his grip got tighter. If he knew about Sebastian, what else did he know? Everything was running through my mind. I started to feel my hand wrap around my glass a little harder as I moved it from in front of me to the side, and before I even thought about it I smash the crystal glass right in to the side of his head.

Harvey's body fell to the floor. I looked at him and saw blood trickling down the side of his face. Stepping over Harvey's body, I made my way to my room but within seconds I found myself being pulled by the ankle causing my weight to crash through the glass coffee table. For a split second I'd lost all my senses, until I felt myself rolling on to my back. Harvey was crouched over me, the blood now dripping off of his face into my hair. It was not until he straddled himself on top of me that I realised I was being pushed into broken glass.

'I know about the gun. I know about the money in your bag. Now tell me! Who is Sebastian?' He pushed my shoulders harder into the broken glass. Harvey's face was unrecognisable. Every ounce of patience had left and been replaced with burning rage. I tried to push back but he was way too strong for me now. Whatever he put in my drink had worked.

'You're meant to be a private detective Harvey! Do your job!' The words left my mouth and I knew I'd made a mistake when he bowed his head down laughing before looking up and slapping me hard. The signet ring he was wearing on his pinkie finger stung as it met my face. Despite Harvey starting to move off of me, I was still lying in the broken glass, though thankfully the room had stopped spinning.

Harvey walked back over and crouched down beside me. I managed to slowly pull myself up.

'Oh honey. Grandpa really set you up didn't he?' His patronising tone really made me want to punch him in the face. I stood up noticing a persistent pain in my ribs.

'What are you talking about?' Harvey started to laugh to himself. He saw that I was confused and laughed harder.

'There is no lead Katheryn! There never was. Your dearest Grandpa set you up.' My whole body went numb.

'But why? Why would he do that? He said I could look for Charlie?'

'Did he though? Or did he just want you out of his way?'

Harvey cupped his hands around my face and looked at me like I was a child. I tried to read his face as if to guess his next move. I reached up to wipe some blood that was about to drip into his eye, smoothing my hand back down over his cheek and with one swift move I lunged my knee into his crotch, instantly disabling him back to the ground. With my coast temporarily clear, I finally made it back to my bed. With my back to the living room, I grabbed my phone out of my bag and called Sebastian but as soon as he picked up the phone was slapped out of my hand.

'Don't you dare.' I turned around and see Harvey.

'Harvey, just let me leave. I won't say a word about what's happened. I won't even go back to New York. I'll stay in Nevada if you want so you can keep track of me. Just let me leave this room.'

'I can't trust you Katheryn. You know that don't you? I can't just let you leave. Your Grandfather gave strict instructions to look after you.' I scoffed.

'Look after me? You think this is looking after me? You touch me up in the back of your car, you have staff at the hotel go through my belongings, you spike my drink and you push me into a glass fucking coffee table?

Are you fucking kidding me?' I tried to push him back but he just stumbled.

'Fine. Go.'

'What?'

'Don't question me. Just go.'

Harvey's defeated. Have I done that? Have I actually managed to defeat Harvey Fersnby?

I grabbed my bag and swung it onto my shoulder before grabbing my phone off of the floor and chucking it into my bag. I walked to exit the bedroom but Harvey was standing in the way. There was silence until someone walked into the room.

Harvey turned to look. It as the young man from earlier, the Turndown Guy, who did a shocking job in turning anything down. My suspicions grew as I noticed Harvey smirking as he turned back around to face me. We were still stuck in silence, I started to feel paranoid. Turndown Guy was just standing a few steps behind Harvey. Things slowly fell into place. I hadn't defeated Harvey at all.

'What do you want from me Harvey?' Now I was the one that sounded defeated.

'I want the $20,000 dollars that you have stashed in your bag' He gestured with his head, nodding it towards my bag. 'It's not like you're going to be without, your precious Sebastian has money waiting for you.'

Wow, he even read my texts. I stared at the Turndown Guy. He shuffled closer towards Harvey.

'Fine.' I reached into my bag, bypassing the rolls of money and placing my hand around the gun instead. Before lifting my hand out of the bag, I stared at Harvey. I never wanted it to come to this. I took a deep breath and pulled the gun out of my bag and aimed it directly at Harvey. He initially stepped back and looked startled before he steadied himself. He smirked.

'Really? You're going to shoot me?'
I kept my eyes set on Harvey, not breaking eye contact., I reached up and pulled the hammer back. The second I did, his whole demeanour

changed. Perhaps tough ol' Harvey gets a bit frightened when the shoe is on the other foot?

'Katheryn, put the gun down. You don't know what you're doing.' Harvey's voice shook slightly.

He was right, I didn't know what I was doing, but I did not trust anyone in this room. I needed out.

'Who's this?' I flicked my gun towards the Turndown Guy.

'That's Joe. Joe Coyne. He works for me.' I rolled my eyes at Harvey's words.

'Of course he does. How long for?' I stared at Joe while commanding Harvey's attention. He was visibly scared, he can't have worked for him for long.

'Three months.' Harvey replied. I sighed.

'Joe. You can leave. I want you to leave, go and get out of here. You deserve better.' Joe looked towards Harvey as if for permission. He slowly walked back to the front door before Harvey turns and grabbed Joe by the wrist and pulled him close to his chest, putting him between the gun and himself.

'Harvey! Don't do this. Don't be a total dick.' I lowered my arm holding the gun to my side.

'I'm not the one holding the gun Katheryn.' I couldn't help but laugh at the words coming out of Harvey's mouth, which didn't seem to make the situation any better. Harvey was getting increasingly agitated.

'If you just give me the money sweetheart, we can all go. You can go, no strings attached.' Annoyingly, Harvey had a good point. What am I doing? Here I was holding a gun to someone who just wanted my money. Though that someone was the person who drugged me and sexual assaulted me in the back of his car. Scratch that. He deserved this.

I regained my composure and lifted the gun back up aiming for Harvey, looking at him without hesitation.

'Let Joe go and you have yourself a deal.'

I stayed completely still as if nothing was said. My eyes darted back and forth between Joe and Harvey, the gun still firmly aimed at his head. I could see Harvey getting agitated, tiny beads of sweat forming on his brow, yet I was completely frozen. I couldn't help but replay everything that's got me here.

My moment was interrupted when all of a sudden Joe was thrown to the floor and I saw Harvey lunging towards me. He tried to push the gun out of my right hand, causing me to fire a bullet into closest wall. I turned to look at Joe and he was on the floor, startled.

'Joe! Run!' I shouted at Joe and as soon as I did, I brought the gun yielding hand up to hit Harvey in the side of his head, just to get him off of me. But he knew now. He knew my every move and he launched his arm up in protection, causing my hand to hit harder than expected. I shut my eyes tightly as another shot was fired.

Something felt different as soon as I heard the bullet being fired. I could feel my whole body deflate. I looked directly into Harvey's eyes and he was looking back, yet the way he was staring at me seemed as if he had heard this kind of gunshot before.

He backed off of me and turns around towards the door. I dropped the gun onto the floor and slowly walk to where Harvey was standing. A part of me hoped the bullet just went into the back of the sofa. I was out of luck.

All I could hear was Harvey's breathing and all

I could see was Joe.

Joe who was just trying to leave.

Joe who got caught up with the wrong crowd.

Joe who must have been only 19 at least. Now

lying with a bullet in his head, and I was the one

who put it there.

# CHAPTER SIX

It was in that moment, when I was staring at Joe's body that I realised I didn't ever want to kill anyone. Not even Harvey. I just wanted the chance to get out and maybe, just maybe, I thought if he was threatened he might ease up and let me go. I never thought I would end up killing someone. Said the girl with the loaded gun.

It feels like hours have passed since Harvey and I spoke. We're both still looking at the lifeless body in front of us. Harvey's breathing starts to become more and more intense and I, without knowing, have started to cry. Those silent tears that seem to just fall out of your eyes. I attempt to compose myself, but before I do Harvey breaks the silence.

'You killed him.' His voice was soft and quiet but as he turned to me I could clearly see the anger penetrating through his eyes. I tried to think of something to say but my body felt like it was stuck in concrete. I immediately turned away and picked my bag up, clutching it close to my chest. I swiftly walked around the body lying lifeless on the floor making sure I didn't add to any evidence they had of me being here.

'Don't you dare.' Harvey growled from across the room. I just laughed, turning the handle of the door.

'If you run now you will never be able to get away from this. This isn't some mistake you can do over Katheryn. The chaos will keep following you, and you know damn sure I will be there when it catches up with you.' The smile faded from my face as the realisation of what I'd actually done seems to finally hit. I looked down briefly with my eyes landing on Joe's face and for a second I felt like I was suffocating. My grip on the door handle got tighter until my hand went numb.

'I'm sorry.' I looked up at Harvey and I had no doubt in my mind that he'd stick to his word. I slipped out of the hotel room and made a beeline for the elevator.

The hotel was almost empty as I walked through. Catching sight of the large gold clock hanging behind the reception, I noticed it was almost 4am. I could not remember the last time I had any proper sleep. I smiled politely at the woman behind the desk as I made my way out of the hotel and down the road.

The roads were quiet and only a few cars passed by. I looked behind me and I could see the faint glow of the main Las Vegas strip glaring up into the night sky. Deciding to avoid the commotion, I started walking straight ahead down the concrete avenue even further away from any kind of civilisation. Within 15 minutes of walking, I stumbled upon a tiny rundown motel. The classic American motel like you'd get in the 50's, with the big neon signs and the Cadillacs outside. However, the big neon sign was no longer working and the Cadillacs had been replaced well, with nothing. It was just a dusty carpark with a flashing sign in the window letting me know they had room vacancies.

As I walked through the door, there was a little lady sitting behind the desk, her silver hair rolled away from her face. Her glasses were the first thing I saw peeping over the edge of the pastel blue desk. I let the door close behind me and I could feel her eyes observing every part of me, not necessarily in a judgemental way but perhaps in a 'would you look at this girl, she's certainly not from around here' kind of way. I became sheepish as I bring myself forward to the reception, her magnified eyes widen as I began to talk.

'Hi, do you still have a room available?' The lady's eyes softened as I asked my question, admiring her black and white uniform I noticed her name tag, Doreen.

'Why yes, we do darlin', how long you staying for?' Doreen's thick southern accent filled the tiny reception area. Now who's the one that's certainly not from around here?

'Just one night please. Is there any chance you have a phone charger going spare? I'm sorry, I just really need to call someone.' Doreen's face flooded with sympathy, her whole face softening as she took in my dishevelled appearance and leant a little closer over the desk.

'Sweetheart, calm down. Look at your poor hands, you're shaking. I shan't ask why a young girl like you is coming and looking for a place to stay at four thirty in the morning or why you have blood seeping through your shirt, but go to room number 4 and I'll come along in a bit with some things. Though don't go braggin' about this, this ain't no common occurrence! Just remember to pay when you leave.' Doreen slid the key across the desk, giving me a wink. I quickly took it and swiftly made my way to room 4.

The room was certainly not going to win any kind of interior design award, but it had a bed and it had running water. I chuck my bag onto the single bed and head straight for the bathroom. The fluorescent lighting did no favours to my appearance staring back at me, but Doreen was right, I had blood on my shirt.

I lifted my shirt up and that's when the pain began to register. I ran my hand over the wound on the left-hand side of my torso and it was rough like grit. Looking down I could see tiny shards of glass embedded into my skin and, with that, the feeling of Harvey pushing me into the broken glass came flooding back. I covered myself over and ran the cold tap. I was too tired to have a shower. I splashed the water over my face, rubbing away at my skin as if I wanted it to come off and somehow reveal some kind of new me. Someone that hadn't just commit a murder. I rubbed away at my face as if I was looking for some kind of answer to all of this, that maybe if I just kept doing this everything would stop. A knock at the door stopped me from carrying on. I grabbed the only towel hanging on the wooden rack, drying my face as I went to answer the door.

'C'mon let me in, let me in!' Doreen had pushed her way into the room before I barely opened the door. She was shorter than I thought she'd be, but clearly made up for that with feistiness. She sat on the edge of the bed, placing a small basket on the bed and beginning to unpack the items. I sat down next to her.

'Now here's the phone charger, and I've found some shampoo and shower gel samples out the back. We don't usually give these out, but here, take them. Oh! I thought you might need these..' She handed me over some medical dressings and some anti-bacterial wipes. I smiled at the thought of her caring so much.

'Thank you Doreen. Could I ask another favour? You can say no, it's just I don't think I can do this myself..' She moved forward and placed her hands on top of mine.

'Of course darlin' what is it?'

'There's glass stuck in the wound and I can't bear to look at it. Would you mind trying to get some of it out? I know that I'm asking a stranger to do something quite intimate so It's fine if you say no, no pressure.' Doreen tapped my hand 3 times before standing up in front of me.

'Go to the bathroom, drawer under the sink, there should be some tweezers next to the mini sewing kit. Don't ask me why we have them, though I suppose now they're coming in useful.' I immediately took her instructions.

There was something about Doreen. A vibe. An aura. Something I was drawn to. Something that made you feel instantly safe. Yes, I'm fully aware how that's gotten me in trouble before, but this feels different, it feels maternal. It could be the fact that I'm 100% sure she bathes in Chanel Mademoiselle or it could be the raspy southern accent that coats every word, but either way she's the first person in days I've felt comfortable around.

Grabbing the tweezers from the drawer, I trundled back over to the bed where Doreen had laid out the towel across the bed.

'You gonna tell me your name?' Doreen almost startled me with how abrupt she was, grabbing the tweezers out of my hand.

'Rose. Rose Delaney' I stuttered. Of course, the first name that came to mind was Sebastian's sister.

I held my hand out for her to shake but she stood there, emotionless.

'And what's the name you were born with? You don't have to pretend with me honey.' I stared back at her briefly before replying.

'Katheryn, but you can call me Kate. How did you know I was lying?'

'You paused to think about it. Then you stuttered. Now lie down.' Doreen's perception astounded me. I lay down on the bed, lifting my shirt up to reveal the wound. Doreen walked to the side of the bed, peering down to take a look, her glasses edging closer to the end of her nose. If it wasn't for the pearly chain holding these glasses around her neck, they'd have fallen off by now.

'You've got yourself into quite the mess, haven't you?' I exhaled heavily as I felt Doreen wiping the wound with a wipe. The stinging sensation subsided quickly, until I felt the cold metal of the tweezers pinch at my skin. I closed my eyes to distract myself and within a few minutes, Doreen's voice broke the silence.

'One more wipe clean and then I'm just going to cover it with this medical dressing.' After a few more uncomfortable minutes I sat up and thank Doreen.

'If you're going to have a shower, try not to get it wet, but you're all set for a day or so darlin.'

'Thank you so much Doreen. While you're here, how much do I owe you for the room?' Doreen looked back at me with a smile on her face.

'Don't worry about it sweetheart. Stay here for as long as you like.' I could feel my eyes welling up as I stared back at her with awe.

'Doreen, are you sure? That means the world to me.' She smiled sweetly.

'Let's say no more of and get some rest. Sadly, I can't offer you breakfast but I'll pop by in the day to check on you' With a small squeeze of my arm, Doreen left the motel room walking back to the reception. I closed the door behind her, ensuring I double locked it just to calm my anxieties.

I finally started to feel a little calmer. Almost like the seas had stopped thrashing my body. I couldn't help but feel slightly dumbfounded at the same time. At a loss for everything that had happened and how I had managed to get myself into this situation. Maybe if I wasn't a Simmonds girl, this wouldn't have happened. Could I blame being born into a rich, power hungry family for my downfall? Could I blame the murder of an innocent man on the fact my family were a bunch of narcissists? Was I the narcissist? I'd been so hung up on finding my brother, thinking I had the right to get involved, thinking that he must want to be found that I went so far that I killed someone. My whole life I had felt an outsider, that I didn't fit into the family, when in reality I'd been a Simmonds all along. Entitled, rich and a massive fucking Narc.

A multitude of vibration noises snapped me from my self-obsessed thoughts. Doreen must have plugged my phone in for me. Picking it up from the side table, I saw 32 missed calls from Sebastian. I dropped down onto the bed scrolling through the 25 messages from him. An abundance of 'What's going on?' 'Kate are you ok?' 'You're scaring me!' 'Please answer your

phone' and the very last message, 'I love you'
sent my heart straight up into my mouth. I could
physically feel my brain going into overdrive
and I tried to calm myself down, but before I
could even start my phone began to ring.

'Sebastian?' I almost whispered his
name as if I didn't believe it was him.

'Kate? Are you ok? Where are you?' His
New York accent was like a comfort blanket to
me, it took me a little while to reply as I could
feel that all familiar lump in my throat trying to
choke me out.

'I'm ok, I'm sorry I haven't contacted
you. I'm in a motel outside of Vegas.'

'Kate, what's happened? You called me
earlier. I heard fighting, are you safe? Is Harvey

with you?' As soon as those words leave his mouth I started to cry.

'Kate? Are you crying?' I couldn't get any words out to communicate, the tears were flowing thick and fast and I couldn't even catch my breath. There was a beeping on my phone and it was Sebastian, trying to FaceTime me. I accepted gladly and there he was.

It must be about 8am in New York. I could tell from his face, still sleepy but immaculately dressed for work. Though not every day was his face this furrowed with worry. Seeing his face made me cry even more. I missed him. I tried to wipe my face and get my breath back and his face softened a little.

'I don't want to make you late for work.'
He stifled a little laugh.

'Don't you worry about that. I want to know that you're safe, because you're not convincing me that you are.'

'I am now. I'm staying here for a little while.'

'What do you mean *now*? You're coming home right?' Sebastian's constant questioning was making me feel on edge. I didn't think I was ready to fully admit what had happened, though would I ever be ready?

'Something happened and I had to leave. I'm not with Harvey anymore. I'm alone.' Sebastian's whole demeanour changed and I could see his anger levels rising.

'You're in Vegas alone? How do you think you're going to find Charlie with no one to help you? Hang on. What did Harvey do?' I couldn't help but feel a little offended by the fact that he didn't think I was capable of surviving alone, though I guess he did have a point with the whole finding Charlie thing without any professional help.

'Harvey didn't do anything.'

'Don't lie to me Katheryn. I heard what was said. I know he took advantage of you, I know he spiked your drink and from what I could make out I heard a gun being fired. Now is not the time to lie to me.' Fuck.

'I shot the gun Sebastian. I killed someone.' His head dropped as he breathed in heavily.

'You killed Harvey?' Sebastian was expressionless.

'No. A boy called Joe. He was innocent. Completely innocent. I killed him.' Just like that I had admitted it all. My voice didn't shake. I didn't lie. I didn't blame anyone else but myself. I could see Sebastian trying hard not to look too disappointed in me.

'You need to come home. I want you home. You can sell your place and stay with me. Your family don't have my address so they won't know you're back in the city. Give me some time to hand my notice in at work and we can move somewhere else. Start a new life. Just me and you.' His confession took be aback. I wasn't expecting that at all.

'Sebastian, I love you too much to drag you into this. You can't throw away your life for someone who's committed a crime. I won't allow it.'

'You love me?' His innocence burst through the phone screen.

'Of course I do. It's always been you.' I've never been this honest, not even with myself, but it's true. Sebastian had always been the one to stand by me and the one that listened to me even when he had no idea if he could help me, he still tried. He made me feel accepted and normal and like I had a purpose, even if that purpose is to just exist. I was happy to just exist if it meant existing next to him.

'Look, give me 3 more days then I give you my full permission to order me home and we can talk about what you proposed properly, ok?'

'Kate. I'm still unsure about you doing all of this alone. If I were with you, none of this would have happened. I want to protect you.'

'I will be ok. I promise. All I need now is some sleep. It's five thirty in the morning. I promise I'll keep in contact and I'll be home in no time.'

'Alright, but can you do one thing? For me?'

'Sure, what is it?'

'Don't hand yourself in to the police until you come home and we talk about everything, ok? Promise me?'

'I promise. Let's just hope I don't get arrested in the meantime..' Sebastian looks at me disapprovingly.

'Don't make jokes now!' I laughed at him laughing. It was good to see him smiling and it was good to feel myself let go if only for 20 minutes. We ended the call with a 'love you' and promised to stay in touch as much as possible. With that I crawled into bed and drifted off to sleep within seconds of my head hitting the pillow.

# CHAPTER SEVEN

I couldn't have been asleep for any more than 5 hours before I was woken up to banging on the motel window. I woke up slowly and for a second I forgot where I was. The banging moved from the window to the door, until I dragged myself out of bed to see what the commotion was about.

I opened the door slightly as I didn't have anything on but my oversized jumper and

Doreen darted in holding a tray with a plate of toast covered with jam and a glass of orange juice, though this morning there was worry etched over her face. I closed the door but she stepped back and immediately locked the door and pulled the chain across for extra security.

'Morning Doreen, is everything ok?' I tried to take the tray out of her hands but she placed it on the bed and turned to me still looking worried.

'You need to tell me everything. Tell me everything about what happened that led you to come here last night.'

'Are you in danger?'

'Tell me Katheryn,' Doreen snapped at me. I started stuttering, not knowing where to start.

'I got caught up with a man called Harvey. He said he'd help me find my brother. My Grandfather hired him but it turns out he's corrupt. He's not a nice man. We got into a heated argument and he ended up pushing me into a glass coffee table, hence the wound I asked you to clean. I had to leave the hotel where I was staying, it wasn't safe so I walked until I found this place.'

'How dangerous is this man?' Doreen's voice didn't quaver.

'Quite. He has some information about me. Well, about what else happened over the

past 48 hours. He also wants my money.'
Doreen's shoulders relaxed slightly as she
exhaled, looking slightly disappointed at the
same time.

'I don't think it's safe for you here
anymore. I'm so sorry.'

'What? Why?'

'I think he's tracked you down. There's
a fancy car out the front. A man wearing a three
piece suit asked if you were staying here. I said
no, but he demanded he looked at the books. He
flashed a gun, I couldn't say no.' I could feel
the anxiety rising as each word left Doreen's
mouth.

'Did he see my name?'

'No, I didn't book you in. He doesn't know you're here. But if he's as dangerous as you're saying, you might need to make a move.' I started pacing around the small room before walking around to the side of my bed to grab my phone and dropped a text to Sebastian to let him know I was on the move.

'Sweetheart, I'm so sorry.' Doreen's sweet Southern voice broke me away from my phone. I looked over to see her standing by the door, not having moved an inch whilst I paced around her, clutching her arms. I walked over to her and engulfed her in a hug. Her tiny frame allowed me to wrap my arms right around her.

'Doreen, you have done nothing to apologise for. I should have known that he would have tracked me down. I only ever had a small amount of time before he tried to find me.' We break away from the hug and I noticed some tears fall down her face. She started fiddling with one of the gold rings on her finger.

'Take this.' She handed me a gold ring with a Ruby set in the centre surrounded by tiny diamonds. 'I've made a phone call to a man named Frank. He's a close friend, he stayed here for two weeks, years back. He was in a bit of trouble then, but he's sorted himself out and made a whole life for himself. If you make your way into the desert from here and walk over that dune, the other side is a main road. Frank has a light blue car, he's going to be driving by around 1pm and get you to safety, ok? When you get over the other side of that dune, just wait by the road. He'll come I promise.'

'Doreen, you don't need to do this.'

'Yes I do. When you see him, show him the ring to confirm it's you, I didn't say who you were. Just to be safe. I promise you, you'll be in safe hands.' I looked down and we were both holding each other's hands. Doreen patted my hand and brought hers up to my face, cupping my cheeks.

'Pack up your things, take what you need from here and head out as soon as you can.' I smiled sheepishly in response to her instructions. Doreen backed away before turning and unlocking the door. I stopped her before she left the room completely.

'Doreen! Thank you. For everything.'

She nodded in response.

'Take care Katheryn.' She smiled just as a couple of tears dropped down her face., She started to walk back to reception before stopping and turning around, 'If you find this Harvey guy, give him hell sweetheart.'

Perhaps I was kidding myself thinking Harvey would give me at least a day's grace before he would track me down. I probably should have tried harder in attempting a getaway. If it wasn't for Doreen helping me in escaping, I think I would be eyes deep in a panic attack about now. Luckily, I didn't leave much of my things around the motel room, just my phone and a pair of shoes. I grab the things I need and stuff them back into my brown leather bag, after taking some clothes out to put on. I walk into the bathroom to change and to take one last look in the mirror.

I slipped the jumper off and replaced it with an oversized grey t-shirt, pairing it with some denim shorts I had managed to grab on my way out of New York, and my only pair of shoes. I ran my fingers through my hair and tried to braid it away from my face. If I was going into the desert I needed to be at least a little bit prepared. God knew how long this trek was going to take. I looked down at my hands and see Doreen's ring sitting on the middle finger on my left hand. I took it off and held it in my hand for a second. I couldn't help but think she trusted me too much. I couldn't fuck this up. From here on out, if I didn't carry on for myself, I had to carry on for Doreen.

Slinging the bag over my shoulder, I peered through the nets of the motel window. My room was at the end of the corridor meaning I could  see most of the car park. It was completely empty. The only cars I could see were the ones whizzing up and down the main road. I went to unlock the front door and took a deep breath just before I opened it. No turning back now Katheryn. I stepped out onto the veranda and to the right of me I saw a path that lead behind the motel and out towards the main road, giving me a direct route towards the dune that Doreen mentioned. I adjusted my bag slightly and headed down the dusty path.

It took me no more than 5 minutes to reach the top main road. The landscape took my breath away. It was just miles and miles of pure golden sand, with the occasional cactus tree adding to the view. I had truly underestimated the sheer expanse of the Nevada desert and how far I needed to walk to get to safety. As I walked further up the road, the number of cars was becoming more and more sparse, and the view resembled that of a film where the sand met the sky. I was lost in the scenery when I turned around to cross the barren road. A glistening silver car caught my eye. It was hurdling towards me as I stepped out into the road and it wasn't until I had scurried across the tarmac into the sand on the other side of the road that I looked back towards the car that was now slowing down. It was Harvey.

I ran from the main road and straight into the desert. The sand dune was right in front of me and I gave everything I had in me to get up there and down the other side to potential safety. I glanced behind me as I got a third of my way up the dune and saw that Harvey had stopped the car and was just watching me from the side of the road. He had a camera and was taking pictures of my every move. I carried on climbing my way up to the top of the sand bank and it was as if I had appeared from nowhere. A road leading in the opposite direction was just as sparse as the one I had just left but I felt a little hope. Perhaps that's the adrenaline. If Harvey wanted to get to me on this side he would need to drive at least 45 minutes around the desert to get to this part of the road. I allow the momentum I had built up from climbing up the dune to get me back down, but before I knew it I tripped on a hidden rock causing me to tumble half way down.

'Fuck.' I stood up and dusted myself off, noticing I had cut my knee pretty bad. The blood was trickling slowly down and I tried to wipe as much of it away as I could before heading back down towards the road. The all

familiar ache was returning above my stomach,
falling half-way down a sand dune probably
didn't help the wound I already had.

I re-adjust my bag and grab my phone
out to check the time. I have half an hour before
this guy Frank turns up. My knight in shining
armour, apparently. I won't hold my breath.
Setting my bag down as soon as I reach the
edge of the road, there might as well be a
tumbleweed going pass me. As the minutes pass
me by, the sun becomes increasingly hot almost
as if it's burning into my skin. All the while, a
few cars go by with the occasional beep of their
horns just to get a reaction. By the time the third
lorry passes doing the exact same thing at the

other two previous I don't even look up from my phone.

Sebastian responds to my earlier text asking for my location.

'The Nevada desert…?' Without a second passing, he's calling me.

'Are you lost?' I snicker slightly at his abruptness.

'Kind of. Harvey tracked me down, he's after me. Doreen hooked me up with some guy named Frank. I'm waiting for him to pick me up. He's going to help.' I'm exhausted from the heat and I don't think my tone had convinced Sebastian that I'm alright.

'Who's Doreen?'

'She's the lady who runs the motel. She's an angel. Doreen has really helped me out.'

'Can you trust her?'

'One thousand percent.' It was only then I could kind of sense that Sebastian relaxed a little. 'I'll be ok Sebastian.'

'It's not that I don't trust you, I just…this is crazy.' I'll give him 5 minutes before he starts begging me to come home. Though granted, this is *crazy*.

'I know. A part of me wants to come home right now.'

'Then why don't you?'

'I can't. I don't think I can ever come back. Not from this.' Sebastian's sigh came across louder than he thought it did. I was right though. I couldn't go back to New York! Not with all of the ties my family had. I either went to prison or I went on the run. There was no other option. I looked up and saw a light blue car in the distance.

'Sebastian?' He'd been silent for a while.

'Sorry, I need to go back to work.' His bluntness caught me off guard.

'Frank is turning up. I'll call you when I can ok?' As quick as that Sebastian had hung up on me. No goodbye, nothing. I tried to not worry about whatever just happened so I shoved my phone into my bag and stood, edging closer to the side of the road to ensure he saw me.

As the pick-up car drove towards me, I saw it was dusty. Definitely a worker's van but you could tell it as well loved. It didn't seem to be slowing down as it came further down the road and ended up driving straight past me. I panicked and started running after it. Within seconds it came to an abrupt stop. I walked up to the driver's window and saw who I assumed was Frank.

He wound the window further down and apologised. He was wearing a blue linen buttoned shirt which matched the car, a detail I didn't think he planned on. His hair was messy and his facial hair was the well-groomed kind. Frank looked nothing like I expected.

'Are you Frank?' I lifted my hand up to push some loose hair out of my face with hoped he saw the ring. He did.

'Doreen called me this morning, hop in.' I muttered a small thanks and made my way round to the passenger seat. As soon as I sat down, it was clear there is no air con but it was so refreshing to not be sat in the blistering sun. I shut the door and leant to pull the seat-belt on. I could feel Frank looking at me but thankfully he hadn't mentioned the blood on my knee.

'You wanting to end up anywhere in particular?' Frank had a strange accent, a blended accent, a mix between deep Southern and the East Coast. With every word his accent fluctuated between states.

'Wherever you're going. For now.' He smiled at me, changed gear and pulled away. My gaze was transfixed looking out the windshield.

It was silent between us in the car, the noise of the engine was engulfing us both and I was leaning my head against the window. My legs were subconsciously facing away from Frank. Looking out into the landscape, I suddenly jolted upright, causing my driver to jump. I broke the silence,

'I can pay for gas! Sorry, I should have said.' A wave of anxiety hit me as if out of nowhere, like my senses were coming back to me. I felt automatically flustered. I was adjusting myself in the seat and just as I did a sharp pain penetrated from my ribs. I turned to Frank as I winced in pain and he was looking back at me, concerned. It immediately made me uncomfortable and I tried to mask the immense pain that I'm feeling.

'You know, I'm just going to give you some money anyway because you seem like someone who isn't going to take it.' I reached down to where my bag was resting between my feet and pulled out a roll of money. I halved it and placed it on the dashboard. Frank started to laugh at me.

'You really don't need to do that and especially not *that* much.' We passed a sign for a diner and he pointed it out 'Just buy me dinner and we're even.'

'Fine, dinner's on me.' I took the money back off the dash and put it back into my bag. We pulled into the diner and parked up. I undid my seatbelt and reached my for my bag. Frank's voice startled me slightly.

'You can leave that in here, you don't want to be carrying that around with you, seems heavy.' He pointed to the worn leather bag I now had clutched to my lap. I started to stutter again.

'Uh, it's fine. I'd rather just keep it by my side if that's ok.' I left the car abruptly and Frank followed soon after.

The diner was your classic 50's American cliché. Red leather seats, a jukebox, and the waitresses were all dressed to fit the theme. We sat down in a booth located in the centre of the diner. I would be concerned about people overhearing our conversation though the place was empty. We must have been two of the first customers of the day, despite it being the afternoon. I sat opposite Frank and he was already looking at the menu. I picked it up and scanned what was on offer but the pain in my ribs was distracting me.

'Hey, can you order me whatever you're having? I'll be back in a minute.' I stood, slinging my bag back over my shoulder. Frank looked up at me. I could tell he was already suspicious.

'Sure. You ok?'

'I'm fine. Just girl stuff.' He just nodded at me as I walked into the ladies room. I'm such a bad liar.

I walked in and there were two cubicles, two sinks, and a mirror that stretches across the whole of the wall. I absentmindedly walked into a cubicle and locked the door. I put the toilet seat down and sat. I rifled through my bag with the intention of finding some medical dressings but the buzzing from my phone derailed my train of thought. I had one voicemail waiting from an unknown number. In that moment I felt the blood drain from every part of my body. I just knew it wasn't going to be good. I began to play the voicemail and brought the phone up to my ear.

'Katheryn. Meet me at the hotel in the next hour. We need to have a little chat, don't we/ If you don't, I'll have to come and get you myself.'

There was no disputing whose voice that was. I ended the call as soon as I could. What else could Harvey need from me? Hearing his voice again knocked the wind right out of my chest. I know that he's following me anyway. I didn't have to turn up, what's the worst that would happen? He'd tell the police that I had killed someone? I was going to hand myself in anyway. At least that's what I was telling myself. I stuffed the phone back into my bag and walked out of the cubicle. I noticed my reflection, causing me to inhale deeply. In the space of three days I seemed to have aged about ten years. I' got lines where there never used to be lines and my brows were now permanently furrowed. I wiped over my eyes with a splash of cold water, taking my hair out of it's braid as I went. I ran my fingers through my hair, readjusted the bag on my shoulder and headed back into the diner.

Walking back over to the booth I saw Frank sitting there with two massive plates of food, slightly regretting telling him to order whatever he's having. As I got closer to the table, Frank lifted his head up just as he was about to bite into the massive burger, his eyes evaluating my body language.

'All good?' He finally bit into his burger as I sat down. I smiled back at him.

'All good.' Things were not all good. I ate a couple of the curly fries on my plate but ended up just pushing the food around the plate. My mind was replaying that voicemail.

'You never told me your name.' I looked up and Frank was looking at me patiently for a reply.

'Katheryn! I'm so sorry!' Smiling, he held out his hand for me to shake.

'Don't worry. Nice to meet you Katheryn. I'm Frank.' We went back to a comfortable silence before he interjected again.

'I won't pry, but what's a girl doing walking though the desert like that?' That sinking feeling weighed me down into the chair and I found myself subconsciously fiddling with the ring on my finger.

'I, um, just got caught short and Doreen helped me out. I just need to get out of here, nothing exciting.' I could tell he didn't buy it because, well neither did I. He scoffed at my fake story.

'Ah, I see. Well, we've all been there.'
At least he was humouring me. I picked at my
food for a little bit longer until I realised Frank
had already finished his. He leant back into the
seat putting one arm on the back of the booth
whilst he gazed out of the window. I followed
his gaze but there was not really much to look at
out there. The same scenery we'd seen for the
past god knows how many hours.

'What are you running from
Katheryn?' Frank's voice was calm, as it always
had been but there is intent behind it this time. I
looked back at him and he looked like he
wanted an answer.

'I'm not running from anything', I
answered coldly. He scoffed.

137

'Fine. *Who.* Who are you running from?' He adjusted in his seat, sitting square on from me.

'I'm not running from anything or anyone, I'm just here to get by. If I'm causing you trouble I can get another ride. It's okay.' Without missing a beat, he sat up in his seat and leant over the table.

'There's no need for you to catch another ride. It's just I struggle to believe you're not escaping from something when you've barely touched your food, you won't let go of your bag, which for the record I know has a substantial amount of money in it, and there is blood coming through your shirt!' I looked

down and he was right. My wound had bled
through my top.

'Oh god.' I got up immediately and
sprinted back into the toilets. I pushed through
the main door and notice it didn't close behind
me. I turned and saw Frank had followed me
into the ladies restroom.

'What are you doing?' I snapped at
him as I locked myself into a cubicle.

'I'm making sure you're ok.' His
voice surrounded the restroom. He sounded
concerned, to my surprise. I lifted my shirt up
and peeled back the medical dressing Doreen
applied yesterday. I groaned as it tugged at the
wound.

'I'm fine, I promise.' Hardly convincing, Katheryn.

I rustled through my bag and the sound of me peeling back medical wrappers and the occasional gasp of pain leaving my mouth filled the room. I pulled my shirt back down and unlocked the cubicle door. Frank as standing there, looking down at the floor. The squeak of the door got his attention and his eyes dropped back onto my blood-stained top.

'I didn't have a clean top.' He hummed in acknowledgement. I walked over to the sink and began to wash my hands.

'Frank, I'm sorry for snapping.' I grabbed some paper towels to dry my hands and dropped them into the bin.

'Do you want to tell me what happened?' My body tensed up and Frank moved closer to me. He placed his hand on my shoulder and I flinched. 'Take your time.' I sighed.

'If I tell you, you're going to want to get involved. I can't risk another person getting involved.'

'You're right. But that's not your decision to make.' Fuck sake. What was it with people being SO nice? I sighed again and propped myself up on the sink counter.

'My family are complicated to say the least. I found out days ago that my brother was alive after being told for 20 years that he had died in an accident. I was only 3 years old when he died. I barely remember him but we mourn him every year. Anyway, I wanted to find him but my family had other ideas. My Grandpa had me followed back to the secret apartment I was staying in, He set me up with a corrupt private detective and I got myself into deep trouble, so now. I'm on the run. I'm never going to find my brother, I can't go home and I'm pretty sure he's following me.' I think I rambled too much as Frank was giving me a confused stare. His head tilted slightly to the left.

'What's your brother's name?' His facial expression didn't change.

'Charlie. Charlie Simmonds. Why?' Frank's body language changed even if his facial expression didn't. He stood back slightly and cleared his throat.

'Oh. Ok, no reason, I know you don't want anyone else getting involved but at least let me help you get back home. But before we go any further, how deep is the trouble you're in?' I can't help but think he recognised Charlie's name. No one reacts to a stranger's name like that. I jump down from the counter forgetting my injuries for a brief second until they make their presence known. I stand in front of Frank and decide to be honest. What more is there to lose?

'I killed someone.'

# CHAPTER EIGHT

The words just flowed out of my mouth. I need to rein in how comfortable I'm becoming with the fact I've murdered someone. It's stopped hitting me hard in the chest, at least in this moment. Frank however, looked as if he had witnessed said murder.

'Who else knows?' He's blunt and to the point

'Just us. Oh and my…friend back home in New York.' Frank starts pacing back and forth in the cubicle.

'Have you heard from this guy who's following you?'

'He left me a voicemail about an hour ago. He wants to meet me back at the hotel we at were yesterday. That's where it happened.' Frank stopped in his tracks and walked back in front of me.

'You need to get rid of this phone. If this guy is as bad as you're implying then I'm not going to leave you until you're safe.' There it was. That uncomfortable feeling I had recently lost flooding back to me. He didn't want to hand me in. Why was everyone protecting me?

'What do I do? All I wanted to do is find my brother.' My eyes started welling up and I started fidgeting with the ring on my finger again. Frank took my hands into his.

'Hey, it'll be ok. Let's get back to the car and we'll figure this out.' He leads me out of the restroom still holding my hand. We walk past the booth, the food now stone cold. Frank reaches into his jeans pocket and throws some cash on the table as we walk out of the diner.

By the time I sit down in the car I'm crying hysterically. Frank hands me some tissues, a piece of old card, and a pen.

'Here. Write down the number of that friend you mentioned. They sound like you can trust them. I'm going to drive down the road to the nearest gas station and get you a burner phone. You don't need to leave the car, I'll get everything you need, ok?'

I couldn't even reply. My body felt like it was going into shock. Frank started driving back onto the main road as I reached my phone out of the bag along with some money. I wrote Sebastian's number down on the piece of card and held it in my hand until we got to the gas station. I held my hand out with some money, gesturing for Frank to take it.

'Please?' He smiled at me sympathetically, took the money and headed into the gas station.

Sitting in the car, I wipe away my tears with the tissue. I start to look through the photos on my phone and come across one of the first photos taken of me and Sebastian. It was taken on the roof of the Empire Hotel. We went out one evening for drinks and ended up there. The sun was setting so beautifully over Central Park, I remember looking over to the park and he came up behind me, put his arms around me and took the picture of us. One of the only pictures taken of me where I'm genuinely smiling ear to ear. I felt like I was back in that moment up until Frank opened the car door.

'Here you go.' He hands me the phone and I start taking it out of the box. 'I got some snacks for the ride. It's a bit of a ride to my home I'm afraid.'

'How far?'

'Four hours. There's one of my old shirts behind you if you need it.' I reach behind the chair and pull out an old plaid shirt and place it over my legs.

'Thanks. I've set up the burner phone. Do I need to get rid of my phone?'

'No, just turn it off and he shouldn't be able to track you from here on in. The burner phone should have a little bit of battery in it if you want to contact your friend.' I do exactly that and put my phone away. I dial Sebastian's number on the burner phone, it rings 4 times before he picks up.

'Sebastian, it's me. I can't speak for long.'

'What number is this?' My heart sank a little at his tone.

'I'm using a burner phone, I'm calling to tell you to only contact me on this number. Is everything ok?'

'No Katheryn. Things are not ok. The woman that I love is halfway across the country, on the run with some stranger because she's committed a fucking crime that if she gets caught will get sent to jail and I may not see her again. You will literally go down for the rest of your life. On top of that, your Grandfather turned up at my work today asking if I had information about where you were. Why would he come to me for information?'

'Sebastian. I'm trying to sort it out. You were the one telling me to get out of there so we can start fresh, I'm trying to do exactly that.' I sit forward in my seat and see Frank in the corner of my eye glancing over.

'Why does your Grandfather think I know where you are Katheryn?' I feel like I could scream.

'Harvey knows I was in contact with you back in the hotel. He's probably told my family that you know something.'

'Probably?! He interrogated me Kate. He sat me down and threatened that if I was lying to him he would make my life hell.'

'Sebastian! I'm sorry that my Grandfather came to see you but I am trying my best. I can't fix this overnight.' My voice cracks as I lean back into the seat. I don't know what more I can say.

'Kate, I'm sorry I didn't mean to snap, but you need to get back here. You can start to find Charlie properly when you get back here.'

'Yeah, I guess. Look, I have go, I need to save the battery. I'm going to be travelling for the next four hours so I'll text you when I get to Frank's, ok?' I feel completely deflated.

'I still love you, you know that don't you?' Sebastian breaks my heart.

'I love you too.' I end the call and throw the phone down, aiming for my bag on the floor. I turn to look at Frank, who's currently driving with one arm on the side of the door window and the other placed on the steering wheel.

'Where exactly is your home Frank?' Not taking his eyes off the repeating road he answers almost immediately.

'Just outside L.A.'

'What're you doing round here then? That's a long way to commute for work?' I hope he hadn't made this journey just because Doreen called him about me.

'I was in town visiting some old friends. I stayed with Doreen a few years back, she took me in for a few months until I found a proper place to live and start my life. She's like a

Mother to me.' Not once did Frank take his eyes off the road when talking to me. I didn't want to ask any more personal questions as I could see he was getting slightly uncomfortable. Looks like I'm not the only one with baggage.

We had been on the road for about an hour and a half. Throughout that 90 minutes I had been staring at the clock on the dashboard. Harvey's words were ringing round my head and I was becoming increasingly conscious that he would be back at the hotel waiting for me to turn up, and when I didn't I couldn't bear the thought of what he'd do. He knew I was not at the motel anymore, he had those pictures of me scrambling up that sand bank so hopefully

Doreen was out of danger. This was not about me and him anymore. My actions were beginning to affect the people around me. The only people who wanted to help me were now my responsibility to protect. It was my responsibility to not fuck up any more than I already had done.

'Frank?' I readjusted myself in the seat. Thank God these seats weren't leather, otherwise with the combination of the heat and my skin I would have been permanently attached to Frank's car.

'If you want a bathroom break already I'm afraid you're gonna have to wait another hour mate.' Frank is funny. He's also incredibly nice. A closed book for sure but nice.

'Why are you helping me? Any person in their right mind would have reported me to the police.' He laughed at my question and glanced over at me.

'I trust Doreen. She wouldn't have called me telling me a young girl was in trouble for any young girl. And she's right. There's more to this story though isn't there? I'm not going to push but I know that it was self-defence right? Or at least an accident. I know you didn't mean it. Plus, if Doreen didn't do this for me all those years back, God knows where I'd be now. You've got to protect your people. No matter who they are or if you know them or not. Be kind and hope to God you're doing the right thing.' Frank almost left me speechless.

'What if we're not doing the right thing?'

'Then fuck it. At least we tried.' We both laughed. The atmosphere in the car was calm as I tried to get comfortable again. Frank's words seemed to have reassured me.

'Any chance you know what kind of car this Harvey guy drives?' Frank says so nonchalantly. I have no idea. All I know is that it's silver.

'I only know it's silver. Why?' I looked behind and see a silver car trailing us.

'I think that's him behind us. He came out of nowhere about 10 minutes ago. Do you recognise him?' The car gets a little closer behind us and I could see Harvey's face. Smug as ever. I turned back in my seat and put Frank's plaid shirt on, wrapping it around myself.

'That's him.' Frank noticed my body language change. I wanted to cover myself up. If Harvey was capable to wanting to sexually assault me when I was fully covered up then what the hell would he be thinking when I was wearing shorts and a t-shirt. I shouldn't have to think about this. Women shouldn't have to think like this.

'What did he do to you Katheryn?'
Frank sped up. The car wasn't the fastest but it was going as fast as it could without falling to pieces.

'Sexually assaulted me. He also drugged me once we got back to the hotel. I'm fine though.' Why was it I always had to reassure people when I dropped that kind of information?

'Are you fucking kidding me?' Frank slammed on the breaks and pulled over. I checked the rear view mirror and Harvey had done the same thing. Looking back at Frank, his knuckles were almost white from clenching the steering wheel so tight.

'What are you doing Frank?' I tried to get him to look at me but he was transfixed. He eventually turned to me staring straight into my eyes. I could see the anger penetrating through his blue eyes but they were still soft. He looked sorry. I was trying to search his face for an answer to my question but to no avail. Frank opened the door and got out. Shutting it, he briefly leant through the window.

'Stay here. Do not get out of the car.' I shouted for him to come back but he just strode towards Harvey's car. I moved over into the driver's seat and leant my head out of the window. I saw Harvey getting out of his car. Before he stood up, Frank walked up to him and grabbed him by the buttons of his shirt and pulled him out and onto the dusty ground.

Harvey started to get up until Frank punched his jaw straight back to the ground. I gasped at the sheer force as his head hits the ground. Frank kept Harvey to the ground by straddling him and holding his shoulders down. They started talking, barely loud enough to hear.

'You need to stay away from Katheryn.' Harvey started to struggle in Frank's grip.

'Just let me talk to her. I'll stay away, I promise.' Frank's grip started to ease up but as soon as it did Harvey jolted up and headbutted Frank causing him to fall back and onto the ground. Blood was now pouring out of Franks face, I jumped out of the car and ran over to him.

'Frank? Oh my god!' I got him to sit up but he was still transfixed on Harvey, who was now towering over me.

'I told you to stay in the car.' He wiped his nose on his shirt, ruining the linen instantly. Harvey came over and put his hand on my shoulder. Frank jumped up and pushed him away.

'Alright! Alright!' Just let me talk to Katheryn.' Harvey now also trying to clear up his face. It was kind of nice seeing him like this. Hurting. He looked vulnerable and tired. I walked over and stood opposite Harvey, Frank stood protectively between us. I wrapped the shirt around me and crossed my arms waiting for Harvey to say whatever he needed to say.

'I'm listening.' My tone is cold. Harvey deserves nothing more. He replied just the same.

'If you had come to the hotel like I asked, you would know that there is no reason for you to be running.' Harvey edged forward and Frank held his hand out to stop him from getting any closer.

'What are you talking about Harvey?'

The words coming out of his mouth were saturated with deceit. The body. It's gone. It's dealt with. No one knows and no one will know.' Harvey pulled out a gun from the inside of his suit and aimed it towards me. Frank and I stepped back simultaneously.

'Woah, bud! Put the gun down.' Frank stepped in between me and the gun, and tried to reason with him.

'Not nice is it Katheryn? Not nice when the shoe's on the other foot!' I placed my hands on Franks waist and stepped to the side so Harvey could see me. I laughed at him and he hated it. This wasn't the reaction he wanted.

'Harvey. You drugged me and held me hostage because you didn't get what you wanted. You told me I could leave then didn't let me leave. I was never going to kill you. You know that. If you hadn't had tried to tackle the gun off of me, Joe would still be alive. Give me the gun and tell me what you have done with Joe's body.' Harvey lowered the gun. You could tell from his quivering lip that he wasn't made for this. He just wanted to be like his Father. That classic story of fighting for his Father's approval. Harvey's Father may be a conman but I truly believe, deep deep down, Harvey is not. Though he was a sexual predator, for sure.

'My Father has some contacts. I promise you, no one will be after you about Joe.' Harvey's tone had completely changed. He was completely defeated. This time for certain, I couldn't help but laugh at his admission.

'Of course the Fernsby's have contacts in hiding bodies. Jesus Christ.' I shook my head and looked down at the ground until I heard Frank start to speak in a slightly hushed tone.

'Did you say Fernsby?' I looked over at him and his brow was furrowed again, glancing between me and Harvey. It was almost as if he was solving some kind of puzzle in his mind and both of the men in front of me were about 20 steps ahead of me. Harvey was just staring at Frank when he cleared his throat and held out the gun for me to hold.

'Here. Take it, it's yours. It isn't loaded. I have to go. I'm sorry.' I held my hand out and he placed the gun for me to hold. Harvey walked past, back to his car and Frank followed him. I turned to look behind and just as Harvey

got into his car, Frank grabbed him by the

shoulder.

'You're Harvey Fernsby?' Harvey

nodded. Frank's head dropped. Harvey held out

his hand for him to shake. Frank hesitated but

eventually reciprocates. I looked at them with

confusion. It was as if they had come to some

kind of silent agreement. Harvey got into his car

and Frank watched him drive off. He stood at

the side of the road for a while as I made my

way back into the car.


Riffling through the glove box in Frank's car I

found more tissue and an old plastic bag. I

wrapped the gun in the tissue and then wrapped

it in the plastic bag before burying it into my personal bag. Frank finally got back into the car and we headed off. There was tension in the car that neither of us wants to address. I thought that maybe I would at least try to clear the air.

'How's your nose?' I couldn't think of anything else to say or anything else that he'd want to talk about. Luckily he humours me enough to reply.

'It's fine. Are you ok?' I hummed in response. 'We've got 2 and a half hours left, let's not fill it with talking nonsense if we can help it.' I got the hint. I leant my head against the window and closed my eyes with the hopes that maybe I couldn't sleep for the rest of this journey. God help me if I had to be conscious.

I was awoken by light nudges on my shoulder. Opening my eyes, the sun had started to set. We'd parked up in a nice neighbourhood. The street was clean and there was a palm tree every hundred yards lining the sidewalk. I turned and saw Frank looking back at me.

'We're here.' He smiled at me and got out of the car. I opened the car door and in front of me was a small green house complete with its own white picket fence. Frank was standing at the gate and gestured with his head to follow him into his house. His front garden had a large oak tree providing shade over a small table and chairs he had situated in front of the small veranda. I never expected Frank to live here, in a small and perfectly managed home in California.

Walking into his home, the walls were white and his furniture was basic but well kept. You could instantly tell he looked after his belongings. The lounge and kitchen was open plan with a door to the back that lead into the bedroom. I lingered in the middle of the lounge with the uncomfortable tension still managed to follow us home. Frank was in the kitchen and started to move a multitude of dirty plates that were sitting on the worktop into the sink.

'I only have one bedroom, so you can either stay in my room and I'll sleep on the sofa or vice versa, whatever you want.' He walked over to me holding out a glass of water.

'Thank you. I'm fine on the sofa.' I took a sip of water and made my way to the sofa, dropping my bag down on the floor. Frank followed, still tidying along the way. He started talking about ordering pizza. As he was still fluttering around his home, I noticed that along with preening his house he removed a photo frame from the mantlepiece and shoved it in a drawer in the kitchen. I said nothing until I realise he was staring at me waiting for a response about the pizza.

'Oh sorry, yeah pizza, that's fine with me!' He definitely knew I saw that.

'Ok, I'll order some.' He walked back to *that* drawer in the kitchen and pulled out a

menu. Before he dialled the number, I
interjected.

'Could I have a shower please?' He
looked up from his phone.

'Of course, right through there. Use
whatever you like, there are clean towels in
there.' Frank pointed to the door at the back of
the kitchen. I thanked him and walked through.

His bathroom was just as basic as the
rest of his house. It'd got your standard toilet
and basin with a large bath and a boxed-in
shower with a white wooden shelving unit
housing the towels. I grabbed two towels and a
wash cloth off the shelf and undress. The water
was refreshingly warm. I let it run down my

body and as I did I could feel tiny fragments of my stress washing away with it. My mind wanders as I began to wash my hair. Reaching up, I ran my hands through my hair and I felt a tugging sensation across my ribs. I looked down and the medical dressing I had put on was starting to come unstuck from the steam of the shower. I slowly ripped it off and allowed the water to wash the wound.

I turned to face the showerhead and let the water pour onto my face. I grabbed the wash cloth and let it lather up using the shower gel I found on the side. I started scrubbing my body from the shoulders down, the dirt just dropping from my skin. I was starting to feel a bit more like myself. As I stepped out of the shower, Frank knocked on the door making me jump. I grabbed the towel as quick as I could.

'Pizza's here!' Still a little startled, I wrapped the towel around me. I let out a sigh of relief.

'Oh thanks! I'll be out in a bit!' I grabbed the second towel and attempted to scrunch the water out of my hair. It dawned on me that I left my bag in the other room with Frank. The bag with my clothes. Oh Kate. I sheepishly opened the door and before I could step out of the bathroom, in front of me on the floor there was a pile of folded clothes. I looked up and Frank steps around the corner, pizza boxes in hand.

'Thought you might want some fresh clothes. It's just some joggers and a fresh shirt so you can be comfy. I can put your clothes in the wash later. I don't have any women's underwear so I've given you a pair of my boxers, I didn't know if you had everything you needed or not so...' I could tell that he was uncomfortable. I laughed at his last comment. Grateful that he even thought about it.

'Thank you Frank.' He headed back into the lounge and I picked up the clothes and headed back into the bathroom.

I started to get dressed and it quickly became apparent that these clothes drowned me. I tried to use the ties on the grey joggers to tighten them around my waist. Luckily, the fresh red plaid shirt dropped down just above my knees, covering any mishap I could have with the joggers. I scrunched my hair with one of the towels one last time before folding them up and placing them over the radiator. I pushed my hair behind my ears and left the bathroom.

The smell of pizza hit me and my stomach began to rumble immediately. I turned the corner and saw Frank sitting on the floor, his back to the coffee table with the two pizza boxes open and a piece taken from each. I didn't say anything, he hadn't realised I was there. He moved slightly and I saw him looking at two leather folders. The penny didn't drop until I stepped forward and his head whipped around showing me what he was looking at.

'Katheryn. I can explain!' Frank looked at me with tears in his eyes. I felt like I had a cannonball sized hole in my stomach.

'What are you doing going through my bag?' I could barely get the words out, I was stuttering.

'I, um, knocked it and these came out. I was just putting them back.' He turned back to the folders on the floor, closed them and put them back into my bag.

'Frank. My bag was zipped closed.' My feet felt like they were glued to the floor. He started to walk towards me, his hands out as if he was pleading for forgiveness.

'Katheryn, I'm sorry, let me explain.' The closer he got to me the hotter my blood seemed to boil. I could feel the heat coming off of my skin.

'You don't need to explain, Frank. I trusted you and you betrayed that. Why do you need to go through my things? Haven't I been honest enough with you?' He stopped in his tracks as soon as I snapped at him.

'You have and I appreciate your honesty, I just needed to check somethi-' I cut him off.

'To check what Frank?' I raised my voice at him and I could feel my words ricocheting off of the walls.

'To check to see that you're my sister.' Frank's words were quiet. As if he didn't even want me to hear and he was right. I didn't want to hear.

'What the fuck are you talking about?' I looked back at Frank and his whole body language had shifted. He was vulnerable and scared. His blue eyes now filled with tears once more.

'It's me. I'm Charlie.'

# CHAPTER NINE

My vision started to fade. My sight started to go black until all I could see was his face. I could feel my chest rising and falling but no air was entering my lungs. My whole body felt like jelly but I was still managing to stand in the same spot. The words that had just left Frank's mouth were circling through my brain. Frank started to step closer towards me, my whole body started to sway, I closed my eyes.

'Katheryn?' He put his hands on my shoulders and my chest became tighter. I started to gasp for air, clenching my eyes shut.

'I need to sit down.' I muttered the words out and Frank put his arm around me and guided me to sit on the sofa. I felt his hands on my knees. I opened my eyes slowly and saw him crouched down in front of me. He reached for the glass of water on the coffee table and picked it up gesturing for me to take a sip.

'Here, drink some water.' I obliged. I took the glass and my hand was unsteady. He took the glass from me and put it back down on the table. We stared at each other for a while until I broke the silence.

'Why did you say that?'

'Because it's true.' I roll my eyes.

'No. No it's not! You read his file and thought, 'Oh, this'll be good, that'll fuck her right up!' What the fuck is wrong with you?' Frank bowed his head and stood up with a sigh.

'I was reading the files in your bag because the second I picked you up on the side of the road I thought it was you. You looked familiar but I never in a million years thought it would be you. Then we got to the diner and you told me what happened in the bathroom and it broke my heart. It sounded just like our family and then I met Harvey and everything slipped into place. I didn't want you to find out like this.' I felt sick. This whole time he knew and didn't say a thing.

'Prove it. Prove to me you're my brother. Prove to me you're Charlie.' This was my downfall. I had nothing to go off of. I always thought that when I found Charlie it would hit me in the face. I thought I would instantly know who he was and that would be that. I didn't expect to meet my brother and have no idea. Frank heads straight to the kitchen and gets the photo frame he hid earlier on and gives it to me.

'That's us. Mum, Dad, me, and you. You were only little, about two I think, one of our last summer's together.' He was right. That was the Hamptons house we went to in the summer. Mum and Dad were sitting on the edge of the pool and Charlie was in the pool, holding me. I had never seen a family photo like this. We all looked happy. Genuinely happy. Even my Mother looked glad to be there. The lump in my throat started rising until he rushed off into his bedroom, coming back with a box full of paperwork and more photos. He sat down next to me on the sofa and started to rifle through, showing me photos.

'This is the day you were born, and this, oh my god, this one was your first Halloween!' He started laughing and handed me a photo of baby me dressed as a pumpkin.

'I've never seen these before! How come you have them?' He passed me more photos.

'I took them. You were my baby sister, you meant the world to me. You still do.' His voice cracked and he cleared his throat. 'How much do you know about why I left Kate?'

'I know that Mum and Dad lied to me for 20 years. I know that our Grandfather paid you off to keep you away. I know that you're meant to be dead. I don't know why though.'

'Do you want to know?' I paused and he looked at me. This was why I decided to find Charlie right? To find out what happened. Why our family felt the need to lie about him dying. But could I really handle any more of this shit? No.

'Not yet. I need some time I think, all of this is a bit much.' Charlie looked at me and smiled.

'That's ok, I understand. Did you want to look through anything else?'

'I want to know why you changed your name to Frank and what all of that was about with Harvey.' Charlie rummaged through the box on his lap again. Pulling out a few documents, he handed them over to me.

'I had to change my name. I needed to start a new life and if I kept my name, it'd be too easy for our family to track me down and find me.' The documents in my hands were of his name change.

'What about Harvey? Had you met him before?' He sighed heavily.

'Kind of. We were friends I suppose. His Father was friends with Grandpa.'

'Joe is his Dad right? Joe Fernsby.' Charlie frowned at me.

'How do you know that?' I raised my eyebrows.

'Grandpa hired him to help me find you. He told me there was a lead in Vegas, I flew out there and then he told me he couldn't help me so passed me over to Harvey. You know the rest.' Charlie shook his head in disbelief.

'I'm sorry that happened to you.' I shrugged my shoulders.

'It is what it is.'

'Ok, my time for questions. Who's this Sebastian guy?' He looked at me the way I always thought my brother would look at me when asking about boys, humorously protective.

'His name is Sebastian. Sebastian Delaney. He works at the bank.' I got cut off by Charlie.

'How long has this been going on? How old is he? Does he treat you good?' I immediately felt embarrassed, I could feel my cheeks beginning to flush.

'About three years, on and off. He's actually the same age as you. Thirty six. He's the nicest guy I've ever met, and he's really helped me out over the past few years.' Charlie's eyebrows were raised but his face began to soften when he realised he'd taken a little while to respond.

'Sorry, I was just trying to get over the fact that my baby sister is dating someone thirteen years older. Do Mum and Dad know about him?' I had to stifle my laugh.

'No, they absolutely do not know about Sebastian. Imagine if Dad found out I was dating someone older than me! He'd hit the roof! Plus he's the manager for a bank, if Sebastian were to get involved with our family they'd be a massive conflict of interest, eh!' We both laughed. It was nice to have someone who got how twisted my family were. Sorry, our family. The talk of Sebastian reminded me I should message him. I got up and searched

through my bag to find the burner phone. I
dropped Sebastian a text;

*'Hey, I made it to Los Angeles. I'm staying with
Frank for a bit. I'll call you tomorrow. Love
you. K x'*

Probably best for me to not mention the whole
'Frank is really Charlie' scenario over text
message.

'The pizza's probably cold now, shall I
order something else?' Charlie starts to box the
pizza up. I drop my phone onto the table and
grab a slice, stopping him from closing the
pizza box.

'Oh. No, it's fine! I'll eat cold pizza!' I walk back to the sofa, making myself comfortable before he continues the conversation.

'You know, I tried to stay close by for the first year. I lived up in Boston until Grandpa found out. I wanted to be able to pop by and check on you. Make sure you were doing ok. They didn't even let me do that.' I saw Charlie getting emotional.

'Hey, it's ok. I'm not mad at you. I know our family are crazy. Whatever happened, you don't have to justify your actions.' I pulled him into a hug. The vibration of my phone on the table broke us apart. It was Sebastian calling. I grabbed the phone, declined the call, and switched it to silent.

'Don't you want to answer that?'

'It's only Sebastian. I want to spend my time with you. He can wait.' I took a bite of pizza and leant back into the sofa. 'Does Doreen know that you're my brother?'

'She has no clue whatsoever.' I laughed to myself. She was a literal angel.

'Doreen told me that you stayed with her for a couple weeks, a few years back. Was that when you left us?' Charlie picked up and slice of pizza and leant back next to me.

'That was when I left Boston. I had just turned seventeen. Dad had an apartment there, near the harbour. I was staying there, no one knew but him until Grandpa turned up at my door with Harvey's Dad. He gave me a suitcase of money and told me to leave. He wanted me as far away as possible. Mr Fernsby drove me all the way from Boston to Nevada and dropped me in the middle of the desert. So I started walking and stumbled across the motel and found Doreen.' I couldn't help but pick up on the similarities of our stories. Our Grandfather was a dickhead.

'Similar to me then.'

'Yeah. Except, Doreen let me stay, rent free for two weeks. I could have stayed longer but I found out that the Fernsby's own a hotel nearby. Doreen, being the godsend she is, told me to fly here, to Pasedena. Her cousin lived here in this house, I stayed with her until she

passed away. Doreen let me stay here, so now I

rent this place from her.' I couldn't get my head

around the fact that Charlie was seventeen years

old when this happened. I'm twenty three and

this was the hardest thing I've ever had to do,

there was no way I could do this as a teenager.

'Weren't you scared?' We both sit up

simultaneously.

'I was scared shitless. I don't think I

stopped being scared for at least two years after.

I was constantly in fear that Grandpa was going

to turn up or worse. I didn't know what to do or

where to turn. I had no qualifications but at least

I managed to get a roof over my head.' The

words of my next question were on the tip of

my tongue. I was so scared to hear the answer.

'What happened Charlie?' He looked at

me worriedly and placed his hand on my leg.

'Are you sure, you don't have to do this

now.' I put my hand on top of his.

'Please tell me. None of this is making

much sense to me. I still don't understand why

you had to leave.' Charlie stood up, grabbing

my glass off the table and walked into the

kitchen. He refilled it and brought it back along

with another for him. He took a deep breath and

sat back down beside me.

'Ok. Remember the house in the

Hamptons? We used to go there every summer.

The last summer I went, the one where I

supposedly died, I caught Mum and Dad having a massive argument late one night. It was about two or three in the morning, the shouting had woken me up. I remember walking into the kitchen and it seemed like one of their usual arguments. They argued *a lot.* This time though, it was the worst I had seen. I hid behind the wall connecting the dining room to the kitchen and overheard everything. From what I understood, Dad had had an affair. Multiple times. With the Nanny, our Nanny.' Charlie grabbed the glass off the table and took a sip.

'Well, that would explain Grandpa paying Mum to stay married to Dad right?' Charlie nodded.

'How do you know about that?'

'I found out on my fifteenth birthday, I had a party at home. Mum and Dad didn't talk to each other the whole night. They ended up having a heated conversation while everyone was singing Happy Birthday to me. Later on that evening I saw Mum and Grandpa walking into the office so I followed them and listened outside the door. All I heard was that Mum was getting paid to stay in the marriage and that Grandpa was the one coughing up the cash.' Charlie looked at me sympathetically again.

'Well, the thing is. This affair that Dad was having started about 36 years ago. A year after Mum and Dad got married.' All of a sudden I could feel my brain imploding. Thirty six years ago?

'Wait. He had an affair while Mum was pregnant with you?' Charlie shifted in his seat, he started rubbing his hands together, like some kind of nervous twitch.

'Kate, Mum was never pregnant with me. Thirty six years ago, Dad had an affair with this woman and got her pregnant. Grandpa and Mum eventually found out and because of the family's connections and how well the business was doing at the time they couldn't risk this getting out and ruining the family name, so they came to an agreement. It was agreed that they would hire her as the Nanny and Mum and Dad would raise me as their own.' I had so many questions but I was completely speechless.

'Nanny Jones? Nanny Jones is your Mother?' I didn't realise how loud my words were until Charlie started hushing me.

'Yes, Kate I'm sorry.' I immediately pulled Charlie in for a hug and I held him as tightly as I could.

'No! I'm sorry. I'm sorry for all of this.' I pulled away. 'Is that how long they've been paying Mum to stay?'

'No. The thing is Kate, he got her pregnant again a few years later and Mum threatened to leave but by this time we had moved to the Upper East Side and everyone knew who our family were, like it is now. So that's when Grandpa started paying her every month as an incentive to stay.' My head was starting to physically hurt from all of this information. I grabbed my drink and downed the whole glass of water in one go wishing it was something stronger.

'So we have another sibling? That doesn't explain why they had to fake your death Charlie.' I rubbed my eyes repeatedly and cupped my face with my hands.

'Kate. You're the baby.' I laughed loudly in Charlie's face. He'd got to be winding me up.

'No, you're joking with me right now. You're lying.' I got up and started to pace around the room.

'Katy, I know this is hard, but I wouldn't lie to you about this. Take all the time you need, I'm here but this is the truth.' Charlie

was sitting on the edge of the sofa watching me

pace back and forth in front of him. I started to

get angry.

'This doesn't explain why they had to lie

about you being dead though. This is so fucked

up.' Charlie stepped across the room and stood

in front of me, stopping my constant pacing.

'Sit down and I'll finish the story.' He

tried to grab my hand to bring me back to the

sofa but I pulled it away from his reach.

'Go on then.' All patience had left my

body but I might as well let him finish the story,

even if I was finding it hard to listen to.

'The night they were arguing was the

night I found all of this out. I was angry too.

Just like you. They never wanted us to find out, they just wanted to carry on with the image of being the perfect happy family. You had woken up from all of the shouting so that's when Jones came downstairs to make you some milk to get you back to sleep. We all stood in silence until she went back upstairs to look after you. Mum and Dad explained everything to me, then and there. How she was our Mother and how I couldn't tell anyone about this. I was so upset. Everything I had ever known was just thrown up into the air. Nanny Jones came back downstairs and sat with us. I couldn't look at her. I told her I didn't want her near me. Like all of this was her fault. I told Mum and Dad that I hated them. I told them that I wished they were dead.'

'Charlie.' A few tears started to fall down his face. He wiped them away almost instantly.

'I didn't mean it. I was just upset. I was sixteen for fuck sake. I stormed off back to bed. I didn't sleep a wink, but when I went to breakfast later that morning, Grandpa was there. He had driven up, no doubt because Mum ordered him there.' I chuckle. That's Mum all over. It's all starting to make sense, she's so far up my Grandfather's ass.

'You don't have to carry on Charlie, if it's too much.' He shakes his head.

'No it's fine. Grandpa offered to take me for a drive that afternoon, so that's what we did. Just me and him. About ten minutes in he starts talking about my trust fund and how he'll let me have access to it early. I told him I didn't want it. He immediately got angry. He pulled the car over and told me that he knew that I knew about the whole situation. I had my suspicions about him for a while but, after that night, it was all confirmed so I decided to threaten him to see how far he'd go.'

'What did you say to him?'

'I told him he'd have to kill me to stop me from saying anything.' I gasped a bit too sharply and hurt my throat.

'Jesus Christ, Charlie.'

'He wouldn't kill his grandson though. Not the heir to his multi-million dollar business. We drove back to the summer house and we all had dinner as usual. That night though there was another argument. Grandpa got involved and tried to fire Jones but she refused to leave. She threatened to sue us and take you if she had to leave and, of course, we weren't going to let that happen.'

'She wanted to take me with her?' Charlie just nodded his head.

'She tried to, actually. In the early hours of the next morning she packed all of her things and got you out of bed and tried to leave. Mum stopped her before she got away.' Charlie started to move around in his seat again, playing with his hands. He cleared his throat, his facial expression was worrying me.

'What is it Charlie? What happened.' He stopped looking at me and stared down at the floor.

'I was watching from my bedroom window, it overlooked the pool. Mum was trying to wrestle you off of her. She got hold of you but Jones fell backwards and hit her head. I ran downstairs to go and help her. I got out on to the patio and Jones was getting up off of the ground., All I remember was seeing her hand covered in blood where she had checked the back of her head. She started to walk towards Mum and you, but Mum kept on telling her to stay away. Jones started to beg and that was when it happened. Jones started to lose her footing, she was swaying and I stepped out to help her but by this point Dad and Grandpa were outside and Dad stopped me. Jones passed out and fell into the pool. No one helped her. I was screaming for someone to do something but they all just watched her drown.'

I put my head in my hands and started to sob. I didn't know what I was sad about most. The fact that literally from the day I was born people had been lying to me or the fact that Charlie went through all of this. I always thought my Father was the good guy in the family. Turns out my parents are just as immoral as each other. Charlie started rubbing my back to try and calm me down.

'That night, I demanded the money from my trust fund. Grandpa refused, he said if I took it when he asked initially there wouldn't have been this problem. I threatened to go to the police about everything, so Dad took me aside once the others went back to bed. He gave me $30,000 of his own money, the keys to his secret apartment in Boston, and told me to leave straight away. He said it was for the best and that I shouldn't come back. I was furious with him. I couldn't bear being there, so I went. I said goodbye to you while you were sleeping, packed my things, grabbed a few photos and I left on the next flight out of there.'

I fell back into sofa and exhale heavily. I felt
sick. I wrapped my arms around myself and I sit
in silence for a bit. Charlie started to tidy away
the photos and documents back into the box as
if nothing had happened, though thankfully
noticing that I didn't really want to talk for a
while. He disappeared into his bedroom and
came back with his arms full of bedding. He
placed it down by the side of the sofa and sat
back down next to me. He didn't say anything,
just grabbed another slice of cold pizza.

'Did you just go along with the fact they
lied about you dying?' My words seemed to
linger in the air.

'I didn't know they were telling people I was dead for a year. Up until they showed up at my door in Boston I had no idea. I promise you. That's why I had to change my name.'

'Why did they though? They could have said anything. They could have said you had gone travelling, why did they tell everyone, including half of New York city, that you were dead?' Charlie scoffs at me and looks at me like I'm an idiot.

'Well, how else would they cover up a dead body in the pool? Better to say it's mine after an innocent accident than the body of a woman who the heir to the Simmonds empire was having an affair with for over thirty years. With Grandpa's contacts and him getting the

Fernsby's involved, no one is going to ask questions. Too much money holds way too much power.' I rolled my eyes knowing full well what he meant. Though the fact that my family, our family, more specifically our Father, would rather lie about their son dying than admit he had an affair, was sitting quite uncomfortably.

# CHAPTER TEN

The oak tree outside Charlie's home was so large that as soon as the sun set the house became encased in darkness. Not that it matters to me as I didn't get to sleep. I was lying flat out on his sofa, which was comfier than I expected but my mind just wouldn't switch off. It was almost as if my body had gone into shock. I was exhausted and my bones ached. Was this the physical effects of trauma setting in? Maybe I was just fucking tired. Or maybe it was

Charlie's snoring coming through from the

other room keeping me awake. I turned onto

my side and saw the box of photos sitting under

the coffee table. I leant and pulled the box

closer to me, taking off the lid. I sat up and

brought the box onto my lap. I sorted through

the three photos he had, bringing the one of all

four of us in the pool to the front. If I closed my

eyes and thought hard enough, I could almost

imagine what life would have been like if none

of this would have happened. What would

happen if things just stayed the same, if no one

had to be paid to stay or paid to stay away.

Would things be fine and normal? Or would we

all just find out eventually?

My body was nudged awake and my eyes opened to blinding light. Charlie was standing over me with a cup of coffee and a plate of toast. He put them down on the table that now only had my phone sitting on top and reached over to me to take the photo I had clutched to my chest.

'Looks like you fell asleep looking through the pictures.' He took it and put it back in the box, taking it back into his bedroom. I sat up, lifting the cup of coffee off of the table. I clutched the mug in my hands.

'Sorry, I wanted another look. Thanks for the toast and coffee!' Charlie walked in and plonked himself at the end of the sofa. I scooched my feet up, moving my knees further up to my chest so he could sit down.

'It's alright, they're there for you to look at. Did you sleep ok? I heard you moving around a little bit.' I took a sip of the hot coffee. It singed my tongue as I swallowed it down.

'Didn't sleep the best, had a lot on my mind..' I reached for a slice of toast but Charlie grabbed the plate for me instead.

'I know it's a lot to take in, all of what was said last night. You can stay here as long as you need.'

'Thank you Charlie. I have a place back in New York. No one knows about it apart from Sebastian. I bought it as soon as I got my trust fund when I was eighteen. I was thinking I might go back and live there. Not alone, but with Sebastian. You're welcome to come too.' He looked at me with those sympathetic eyes again. I was starting to hate that.

'Kate, I can't go back to New York. You know that.' I shuffled closer to Charlie.

'Ok, I thought about this last night when I couldn't sleep. My apartment is in Brooklyn. Our family would never think about stepping outside of the Upper East Side. Plus, it wouldn't be forever. Sebastian and I had already talked of moving elsewhere, to start fresh. Please come with me. At least just come for a couple of days, just to meet Sebastian!' I rambled quickly to try to persuade him.

'Kate. You're forgetting one tiny thing. Didn't you say that Grandpa had you followed back to your apartment? Remember when we were in the toilets at the diner, when you told me everything..?' I froze. I completely forgot.

'He has my address.' The words came out as just whimpers. My first thought was Sebastian. I pushed the duvet off of me and Charlie pushed it to the floor, I grabbed the phone off of the table and immediately dialled Sebastian's number.

'Who are you calling?' I turned to him with tears filling my eyes.

'Sebastian. I need to tell him. I'm such a fucking idiot!' The one thing I kept sacred was my apartment. The phone rang continuously and

217

went straight to voicemail. I hung up and that's

when I saw the five missed calls from

Sebastian. All from last night. I dialled his

number again and he picked up almost

immediately.

'Sebastian?' All I heard on the other line

was him sighing deeply.

'Kate, I've been trying to get hold of

you all night!' His voice was panicked, I started

pacing again.

'Sorry, my phone was on silent. What's

going on? You sound stressed.' Before I even

finished my sentence he started his.

'Your place has been broken into. I was

trying to let you know last night. I went over to

pick up some shoes I left there and the door was

busted in.' I looked at Charlie who was now standing in the kitchen leaning against the sink watching me pace. I brought the phone down and muffled the mic.

'They've broken in to my apartment.' Charlie mouthed a 'fuck' towards the ceiling as I brought the phone back up to my ear.

'Seb, was anything taken? Are you hurt?'

'I'm fine honey. I've had a look around, I can't tell if anything has been taken but I'm not sure, everything is all over the place. They've turned the place upside down. Is this something to do with your family by any chance?' I felt a sharp pain in my chest. It pained me to hear Sebastian talk so innocently sometimes. I hated myself because he did so much for me but I was never one hundred percent honest with him. I told him drips and drabs of information but never the whole story, yet each and every time he always did the most. I didn't deserve him at all.

'Yes. It's my family. It's my Grandfather. Don't call the police. I'm going to come home.'

'No you're not! You're going to tell me everything. I know you're not telling me the full story, Katheryn. If they are pulling this kind of stunt when you're not here, think about what they'd do if they knew you were back!'

'Sebastian, it's complicated!'

'I don't give a fuck, Katheryn. You told me you killed someone, I didn't run away did I? How much more fucking complicated can it get?' I burst into tears. 'Katy, are you in trouble again?' It was like a floodgate had been opened.

'It's Frank.' I couldn't even finish my sentence before Sebastian cut me off.

'What the fuck has he done to you? I knew you shouldn't have trusted this guy!' His voice bellowed through the phone and it even made Charlie look back at me in shock.

'Sebastian, calm down. He hasn't done anything, it's just…Frank is my brother.' There was silence on the line but I could still hear his breathing.

'You have another brother?'

'No, Frank is Charlie. I found him. Completely by accident but I still found him.' Sebastian begins to laugh.

'You are kidding, right? So you're telling me that you were put in contact with this guy who then happens to be your missing brother. I'm assuming he told you this after you told him why you were on the run?' Ok. I'll hand it to him, it *did* sounds shady as fuck.

'Look, I know it's a lot to take in, I've barely managed to get my head around it, but it's all legit. I promise.'

'Katheryn. I want to believe you, I do but I don't think I can let you go through all this again. I'm coming to California. I'll get the next flight out to Los Angeles.' My chest tightened. I could feel a panic attack coming on. My skin started to get hotter. Charlie noticed and I began to walk backwards to the sofa. He quickly took me by the arm and guided me to sit down. Sitting beside me, he took the phone from my hand and cleared his throat.

'Sebastian, it's Charlie. I'm sorry about this. I think Katheryn is having a panic attack again. As much as she thinks having you here isn't what she wants, I think it's what she needs. Please come out and you can stay here, I'll pick you up from the airport. Again, I'm so sorry.'

'Fuck. Is she ok? It helps if you open a window or a door or something, get a breeze in. If you can, watching *Friends* on loop seems to calm her right down. I don't know if you heard what I said but if you did, I'm sorry. It's just I love her and I care about her and everything that's happened and knowing that there is so much she hasn't told me, it worries me. If anything happens to her, I'll never forgive myself.'

'You sound like a good man Sebastian. My sister is lucky to have you. Get on that plane and I'll see you in six hours.'

'Text me to let me know if she's ok?'

'I will mate.' Charlie hung up the phone and got up to open a window. The breeze hit me in the face like I'd just downed a cold glass of water. My head was in my hands once more and my chest seemed to be getting tighter and tighter. I could hear Charlie's footsteps across the wooden floor going back and forth and the

sound of the television panicked me further just

for a second until that old familiar theme tune

began. Charlie's arm wrapped around my

shoulders once more as he came back to the

sofa. I lifted my head up from my hands and

leant into Charlie's side. We both leant back

into the sofa while my tears slowly started to

stop falling, my breathing only hitching slightly

now.

'Your boyfriend said that watching this

show would help.' I wiped my eyes with my

shirt sleeve.

'It's an old favourite. I always put it on

when life gets a bit rubbish. I think I must have

watched all the episodes about a hundred times each, at least.' Charlie laughed at me.

'If it helps it helps. How long have you been having panic attacks?' I tried to keep my focus on the tv but the question made me deeply uncomfortable.

'I can't really remember. It was maybe about three years ago that someone told me what was happening to me was a panic attack but I think I'd been having them for a lot longer. I feel like I've always had anxiety, it's one of the only consistencies in my life.' That was meant to come out as a funny remark but seemed to settle in the air as painfully true.

'Do you feel like that maybe the secrecy of what goes on with Mum and Dad contributes to your anxiety?'

'I do think it plays a part. It's the fact when I was living there full time, I was constantly walking on eggshells. The house became a minefield. Then I started to leave and spend nights away and they wouldn't even notice I was gone. It fucks you over, stuff like that.' Charlie squeezed me a little tighter.

'I'm sorry.'

'You have nothing to apologise for Charlie.'

'I'll remind you of that when Sebastian turns up in six hours.' I laughed.

'Thank you for making him come. I think it was the idea of him being fully involved and the whole thing with my apartment that sent me off.'

'It's alright, just sit here for the day and chill out. I said I'll text him to let him know you're ok.' Charlie got up and used my phone.

*Hi Bud, it's Charlie. K is fine. If you can could, you bring her a change of clothes please, other than that all is fine.*

Charlie headed into his bedroom. I picked up the duvet from the floor and wrapped it around myself, like I was the filling in the middle of this feather filled burrito. Charlie came back out of his room with a towel and some clothes in hand.

'I'm just going to have a shower. Your phone is on charge in the kitchen if you need it but Sebastian is catching a flight in half an hour.'

'Thank you, Charlie.' He smiled at me and headed off into the bathroom. Within ten seconds of him locking the bathroom door, he started blasting his music as he turned the shower on. I picked up the tv remote off of the table and turned the volume up. So this was what it was like having a brother.

It made me happy as much as it annoyed me. It was the little things I noticed, like the loud music blasting through the wall when I'd got the tv on or the fact that he kept looking at me like I was still three years old or that whenever I talked about my boyfriend he appeared to sound happy for me but there was just a hint of concern lacing his words. All of those things were what I realised I've missed all this time. I'd always thought growing up that, if Charlie was around, things wouldn't have been as tough on me as they were. I'd have had someone there to have my back and not protect me per say, but at least keep an eye out. Maybe that's super selfish of me to say but it's honest. It was hard being the only child left who was undermined and not trusted. It was hard having to prove myself every day. You give up in the end. What was the point of trying so hard when no one was going to listen anyway? The point

was, at least you tried. I tried and it wasn't good

enough for them and that's ok. Fuck their

feelings. I supposed now I could prove to them

that I was capable. They couldn't kill this kid

off.

# CHAPTER ELEVEN

I've spent the last four hours stuck to the couch watching *Friends*. I think Charlie started getting sick of it about an hour ago when he left to go buy groceries. The eighth episode starts just as Charlie walks back into the house.

'Really? Another one! I know it helps Kate but I think I'm going insane!' His desperation made me laugh.

'Ok, ok! You do have a point!' I kick the duvet off and get up, folding the covers and putting it back down by the side of the sofa. I walk into the kitchen and help Charlie put away the groceries, which mainly consisted of bread, cheese, beer, and one bag of frozen peas. I really don't know what I expected.

'Fancy ordering in for dinner tonight?' I look at him thinking he's being sarcastic.

'What do you mean Charlie, we can make a perfectly good meal with all of these groceries you've bought!' He eventually cottons on to my sarcasm, after gawking at me in confusion.

'Look, I have the essentials don't I? Does Sebastian eat Chinese food?' I roll my eyes playfully.

'Yeah, he'll eat Chinese food. We used to have it every Saturday night.'

'Every Saturday?' We finish up in the kitchen and move back into the lounge.

'That's right. I used to sneak out of the house and meet him at my apartment. Sometimes we'd switch it up by ordering Thai if it was a special occasion.' He looks at me in disbelief.

'Are you serious?' I turn square on to him.

'I'm deadly serious, Charlie.' We both erupt into laughter and fall onto the sofa.

Charlie checks his watch and at the same time a beeping comes from a cupboard in the kitchen. He bounces up and fumbles around until he comes back with folded clothes in his hands.

'I put your clothes in the wash. They've just come out of the dryer. All clean and no blood. You're lucky I had some stain remover!'

Wow.

'When did you do that?' I took the clothes from him and they were still warm.

'About two hours ago, I think you were too engrossed in Rachel and Ross making out on the tv screen to even notice I was cleaning up.'

'Ah, thank you!' I gave him a hug.

'I hope you don't mind. I got the other clothes out of your bag too and gave them a wash, I also got Sebastian to bring you some extras, just in case you stay here longer.' I smiled at his generosity. He was turning out to be quite a good brother.

'No that's great, I was dreading having to wear these shorts again!' I headed into the bathroom and began to undress. I made the mistake of lifting my shirt over my head again. I looked down and saw that I forgot to put on a fresh dressing after my shower last night. Luckily, the wound hadn't bled much but I should probably put one on just in case. I shouted for Charlie through the bathroom door.

'You alright?' He shouted back.

'Can you see if I have any more medical dressings in my bag please?' All I heard were footsteps and rustling until the footsteps crept closer to the bathroom door.

'There are none in your bag, you have some antiseptic wipes though. I've got a first aid kit somewhere, hang on.' I begin to undo the buttons on the shirt and slip my arms in, wrapping it right around me. Charlie knocks on the door, I unlock it and open it slightly just popping my head around and reaching my hand out. He hands me a medical dressing and a packet of wipes.

'Thank you.' I shut the door quickly and slipped the shirt off. I took the wipe out of the packet and gently wiped around the wound. It was healing quicker than I thought but it was still sore. The medical dressing at this point was purely for protection, to stop it rubbing on my shirt. I placed the dressing over the wound and slipped my newly cleaned shirt on. Pairing it with my blue jeans, I looked in the mirror and realise I was wearing the same outfit I wore when I left New York. I slung the grey cardigan on and left the bathroom picking up the clothes as I went.

'Shall I put these in the washing machine?' I held Charlie's clothes up to let him see what I was talking about.

'Yeah, just pop them in. I'll wash them later.' I did exactly that and walked over to where he was sitting and put the other clean clothes back in my bag. Clean clothes are extremely underestimated.

'You never told me how you got that injury.' Charlie was calm but his face was saying something else. He was frowning at me. I exhaled and sat down next to him.

'When Harvey drugged me, we got in a fight.'

'A physical fight?'

'Yeah. I smashed a glass into his head when he started pressuring me into giving him information. I tried to walk away but he grabbed my ankle and I feel into the glass table. I tried my best to get up but he got on top of me and pushed me deep into the glass.' Charlie leant forward, his hands clasped together. I leant forward with him and see that his knuckles were almost white.

'Did he hurt you in any other way?'

'My backs a bit scratched up from the glass. He did slap me across the face but that hasn't left a mark. I'm ok though, Charlie.' He turned to me and his eyes had gone from blue to brown in a heartbeat.

'That's not the point Katheryn.' I tried to calm him down by rubbing his back but he just flinched away.

'Don't think about doing anything. You've already beat him up and made him bleed, you don't need to do anything else. I'm safe now.'

'Are you though, Katheryn? Are you really *that* safe now?' He stood up with a huff and walked over to the window.

'Charlie. Please.' He whipped his whole body around and pointed his finger at me.

'You. You never should have started looking for me. Do you know how much danger you've put yourself in? How much danger your putting other people in? You have no fucking idea what you've got yourself into!'

'Hey! Don't you dare. I know what I've done! I know because I was there Charlie. I was the one he drugged, I was the one he sexually assaulted., I was the one who ran across the fucking desert away from him whilst he was taking pictures of me. I know how much danger

I've been in, how much I'm still in, and how much danger I'm putting other people in, but what more can I do? Charlie! Tell me that! If the shoe was on the other foot, what would have you done?' My voice started to break from shouting so much. Charlie's body relaxed as he bowed his head down to the floor.

'I would have done the same as you.'

'Sorry, what was that Charlie? I didn't hear.' He looked up and raised his voice.

'I would have done the same, Katheryn. I'm sorry, I'm just so angry.' I scoffed at his remark.

'You and me both, Charlie. But what's happened has happened. I know I haven't done it perfectly. I've made mistakes, I know that, but I can't change what's happened and it doesn't matter how many people you beat up for me, it still won't change what's happened. Getting angry doesn't help anyone, you just have to accept what's happened, move on and try to not do the same thing twice.' He stared at me and raised his eyebrows.

'You're smart you know that? Stupid, but smart.'

'That doesn't make sense, and that's not a compliment.' Charlie walked over to me and pulled me into a hug.

'Oh shush, you smarty pants. I'm sorry for shouting at you.'

'I'm sorry too. When do we need to leave for the airport?' Charlie pulled away and checked his watch.

'About ten minutes ago. Shall we head off?' My eyes widened. I grabbed my shoes as we headed out of the door and into Charlie's car.

The airport was a half hour drive from Charlie's house. I spent most of the car ride staring at the scenery, thinking about the possibility of living this side of the country. That's a conversation for another time perhaps. As we got closer to the airport my anxieties started to build again. It felt like a mix of butterflies and pure dread circling my stomach. My leg started bobbing up and down as a result.

'Nervous?' Charlie grabbed my attention from staring out the window. I looked over at him and he glanced down at my leg and then back to the road. Embarrassed, I stopped.

'A little.' I started pulling the sleeves of my cardigan down over my hands.

'It'll be alright. He'll come round plus it'll be easier once he's here, face to face, and we can go through the pictures and all of that. Don't worry, Kate.'

'I just don't want him to hate me.' Charlie started to laugh quietly to himself.

'Kate. You've literally told him that you accidentally killed someone and he's still

245

wanting to be with you. He's just flown three thousand miles to talk. I can assure you he doesn't hate you.' I exhale heavily and lean my head back into the headrest. Internally, I was battling my insecurities and questioning why exactly Sebastian choose to stick around but now was not the time. Charlie pulled into the airport and parked up. I cleared my throat and undid my seatbelt.

'I'll go get him then.' Charlie reached over and put his hand on my shoulder before I opened the car door.

'It'll be alright. I promise.' I nodded my head before I jumped out of the car and made my way to the arrivals. There were swarms of people surrounding the entrance of arrivals.

People holding up cards with names on, family members with homemade banners, and then little old me standing there at the back barely able to see over the heads of the others in front of me. Looking at the screen above me, Sebastian's flight landed a few minutes ago so he should have been on his way to get his bags. I looked around as more people seemed to crowd the area around me. Some passengers started to trickle through and names were shouted out amongst the noise of happy reunions. Tears were shed and they moved on. It happened four times before I saw him.

Even though I've only been away for just about a week, I felt like I'd aged ten years. Sebastian, however, seemed to have not aged at all. He almost looked better, albeit a little tired from the flight. He didn't notice me straight away and for that I was grateful. I got to stare at him a little longer without him seeing me. Dark blue jeans, a dark t-shirt with his Ray Bans hanging onto his collar, and the white adidas trainers were what set him apart from everyone else. Not because he was one of the very few people not wearing colour but mainly on *how* he was wearing them. Sebastian had always been a fit man. He was not an avid gym-goer but he tried to make an effort and that shirt was certainly proving that. The next thing I noticed was his face. More importantly, his facial hair.

Sebastian had always been clean shaven. I think the last time I saw him with any kind of facial hair was when he had two weeks off work last year and we went away to Italy. He saw an Italian man in the hotel we were staying at and became obsessed with his beard, so he decided to try to grow his own. Astonishingly to me, it grew pretty quick. Within a week, he had a full beard. I loved it but he had to shave it off eventually for work. Since when was he allowed to have a beard for work?

He starts to walk into the crowd and spots me. I, for some reason jump up onto my tippy toes and wave. He dodges his way through the crowd and, as soon as he gets within two metres of me, I leap forward and engulf him in a hug, forcing him to drop his bags. His cologne brings tears to my eyes and every worry I had seems to just melt away as soon as I'm in his arms. Soppy, I know. He pulls away from the hug and brings his hands to my face, he wipes away the tears with his thumbs.

'Hey, you.' Hearing his voice in person sent more tears streaming down my face. He leant in for a kiss and I happily oblige. Just being back in the moment of kissing him and feeling his hands on my body, I felt safe. I felt loved and, most of all, I felt complete. Do not get me wrong, having a boyfriend did not complete me. I completed me. He just made me feel shinier. All sparkly inside. Happy. LOVED.

I pulled away gently and he leant his forehead against mine. We stayed in this moment for what felt like a few minutes.

'Charlie is parked up outside, do you wanna head off?' My voice was calm and almost came out as a whisper. Sebastian placed a kiss on my forehead and leant to pick up his bags.

'Let's go honey!' I tried to take one of his bags but he insisted he takes them both himself. He slung his large holdall onto his shoulder and carried the other smaller bag with his right hand, his left arm instinctively making its way over my shoulders, pulling me into his side as we walked out of the airport. As soon as we made our way through the doors, a car horn made us jump. We both turned to our left and saw Charlie waving frantically from inside the car.

'That's Charlie!' I grabbed Sebastian's hand and pulled him over to the car. Charlie jumped out and held his hand out for Sebastian.

'Hi bud, I'm Charlie, nice to meet you!' Sebastian reluctantly shook his hand. I looked at his face and he was scoping him out.

'Sebastian, nice to meet you.' There was a weird tension in the air. Charlie looked over to me and raised his eyebrows before clapping his hands together.

'Shall we get going?' Charlie moved round the car and opened the trunk. Sebastian followed and put his bags in while I got into the back of the car, leaving the door open for my

boyfriend, which would have been a nice

gesture if he didn't ignore it. He closed the door

as he walked past and sat in the passenger seat

without saying a word. This was going to be a

fun half an hour. Charlie shut the trunk and got

back into the driver's seat. He looked over at

Sebastian, who was staring back at him. Charlie

cleared his throat and began the drive back

home.

After about 10 minutes of excruciating

silence, I decided to attempt to clear the air. I

leant forward from my back seat and hoped I

didn't get a frosty response.

'How was the flight Seb?' I lingered

forward to wait for a response while he played

with his newly grown beard. Hopefully, he was thinking of a thrilling reply.

'It was fine, thanks.' His icy tone pushed me back into my seat. I didn't bother saying , anything else, I just sighed.

For the next twenty minutes we were back in that all-consuming silence. Every now and then Charlie attempted to spark conversation but was only met with one or two word answers. Thankfully, we pulled up to his house just as my patience started wearing thin. Charlie parked up and removed his seat belt, I did the same.

'We'll meet you in there.' Sebastian addressed Charlie as he also removed his seat belt. Charlie glanced behind to me and I gave him a reassuring nod. He got out of the car,

taking Sebastian's luggage out of the trunk. I

waited until Charlie was inside the house before

I spoke.

'What is all this?' Sebastian turned in

his seat, now sitting almost face to face.

'What do you mean?' His tone was

condescending.

'I mean, the whole, being cold with

Charlie, not engaging and being damn fucking

rude!'

'I am not being rude!'

'Yes you are Sebastian! Have some

respect at least, he's letting us stay in his house.

He doesn't need to do that.' Sebastian dropped

his head.

'I'm sorry. You're right, but I'm still unsure about this guy Kate.' I cupped his face with my hand and he looked up at me.

'I know you are. Just come inside and we can go through everything, together.' I leant in and kissed him gently on the lips. We both got out of the car and walked up and into Charlie's house hand in hand.

As we walked in, Charlie took the luggage through to his bedroom. I slipped my shoes off by the front door and headed into the kitchen to make us all a drink. I expected Sebastian to follow but I turned around and he was still standing by the front door. I went to speak to him but Charlie came out of the bedroom interrupting my opportunity.

'You two can stay in my room, I'll sleep on the sofa. I've put your bags on the bed.' Charlie walked over to the front door where Sebastian was standing and slipped off his shoes.

'Thank you Charlie.' Sebastian's words were quiet. Charlie patted him on the arm and muttered a 'no problem' before joining me in the kitchen. I finished making the three coffees. Charlie took one and I brought the other two over to the coffee table. Sebastian finally sat down on the sofa. Charlie joined him and I sat opposite, on the floor. We each sipped our coffees simultaneously twice until someone piped up.

'Fancy some Chinese food for dinner tonight?' Charlie addressed the whole room, with Sebastian nodding as he took another gulp of coffee.

'Sounds good to me.' I tried my best to fill the silence again, but within seconds we're back where we started. I stared at Charlie and rolled my eyes again. I truly believed that with the amount that I roll my eyes on a daily basis, I might as well just have whites as eyes. My Mother always used to tell me off for rolling my eyes. My excuse was, and always will be, then don't give me a reason to. God, I was a horrible child. The longer I sat on the floor, the quicker it came to me that we were all just sitting and avoiding the elephant in the room. Sebastian was still pissed about me believing a stranger

that he's my brother. Charlie was just awkward

because Sebastian was pissed and I was just

sitting here hoping one of them would just man

up and get the ball rolling. I was getting

increasingly impatient. I slammed my mug of

coffee onto the table in front of me and stood

up. I charged into Charlie's bedroom and

searched under the bed for the box. I pulled it

out and dropped it onto the table.

'Right. Let's start this shall we? Because

if I wait any longer you two will be sat in

silence until the end of time!' I looked at the

boys sitting on the sofa and they were both

looking back at me like deer in headlights. They

turned to each other and then burst into

laughter. I glared at them and soon they stopped. I sat myself back down on the floor, taking a deep breath. I lifted the lid off of the box. I looked up at Charlie.

'So, who wants to start?'

# CHAPTER TWELVE

The past two hours, I think the word 'fuck' was said about fifteen times. All by Sebastian. It was on the second time of explaining that he looked at me with such sorrow in his eyes. Thankfully, Charlie took the lead on everything. The story telling, the photos, and the apologies. I just sat back and watched.

It felt like I was having an outer body experience. I could clearly see it was me in all of these photos and that it was me in the story

that Charlie was telling but I didn't remember

any of it. On one hand, I was grateful for that.

For being so young that I physically could not

remember but, on the other hand, there was a

part of me that wanted to remember. I felt it

would make everything clearer. Perhaps I could

understand it more if I felt I had been there. If I

had actually seen my real Mother's face. It was

all just a story, it didn't feel lived. I knew I was

not the first person to experience anything like

this but if you were me, would you feel the

same? Would you feel like a ghost with no past?

Would you feel lost and betrayed? Because I

did. My life was being told by other people,

being shown to me via photographs, but it

didn't exist to me. This was a horrible feeling.

I noticed the room was getting darker so

I got up and flicked the lights on. All of those

feelings seemed to hit me as soon as I stood up,

like a headrush of emotions. I absentmindedly

walked into the bathroom and locked the door

behind me, without saying a word to the boys. I

sat down onto the toilet seat and breathed out as

if I'd been holding my breath for hours.

Everything was ok when I woke up this

morning, I had something to distract myself

with other than think about what was said last

night but hearing everything for the second time

seemed to be doubly heavy. I knew Sebastian

had so many questions that I just didn't have the

answer to and, deep down, I don't think I wanted to know the answer to. This was the perfect opportunity for me to break from my family. They'd already cut me off and Sebastian had sorted my money out, or at least I hoped so. Even if I have none of my money left, I could just get a job and start as if I was brand new. Do a Charlie and change my name. Relocate to California. Why not? A knock on the door broke me from my thoughts.

'Kate? You ok?' For a split second I forgot Sebastian was there. I stood and looked into the mirror, pushing my hair behind my ears. I unlocked the door and saw him standing against the door frame. 'Did it get a bit much?'

He reached out and grabbed my hand, pulling

me into him.

'A little. It's hard to get my head around

it all.' My words were muffled against his chest.

He hugged me tighter and kissed my head.

'I apologised to Charlie.' I pulled away

and looked at him with my eyebrows raised.

'You did?' He pulled me back in and his

chest rose slightly from stifling a laugh at my

reaction.

'I was being a dick. It was rude of me, I

understand everything now and I'm sorry. To

you too. It was hard being so far away and

hearing about all these things that were

happening and then all of a sudden this guy

turns out to be your brother. It just didn't seem

believable but I know now. You were fuckin cute dressed as a pumpkin too.' I started to laugh and slapped his chest.

'Oh god! I can't believe he showed you that!' I buried my head into my hands. Absolutely mortifying. Sebastian kissed my head once more before I drag myself away, pulling him with me back to the lounge. Charlie was sitting on the sofa, putting all of the things back into the box again. He looked up and smiled at me sympathetically. I took the seat next to him.

'You alright, kiddo?' He stopped what he was doing and focused his attention on me. I sighed but this time I actually felt a bit better doing so.

'I'm ok. It's a lot to come to terms with, a lot to comprehend.' Charlie placed his hand on top of mine.

'I know. Take as much time as you need. Shall I order that Chinese food? Might make you feel a bit better if you eat something? We can put a film on and have a nice chill evening.' I so appreciated him. I saw Sebastian in the corner of my eye, watching us.

'We could watch Love Actually? You love a soppy British love story!' Charlie's gaze darted between us and eventually landed back on me.

'Love Actually is a Christmas movie. It's August. Absolutely not!' Charlie's voice raised about ten decibels. He must have felt strongly about this film. Your honour, Love Actually was a perfect film for any time of year.

'Woah, Charlie! You're acting like we asked to watch A Christmas Carol! We can watch whatever, as long as you go and order that food now! I'm starving!' He dashed into the kitchen and finally ordered the Chinese food. Sebastian sat down beside me and we flicked through the tv looking for a film to watch. My mind began to wander again. My mind couldn't seem to focus, as if the second I was not preoccupied by something else everything about the past week muddied my brain. At this point, fuck what Charlie told me about the past. Fuck the fact my Mother wasn't my Mother. I didn't think Harvey was telling the truth about letting me go. Why would he get

his Dad's contacts to help getting rid of a body?

That kind of information would surely get back

to his Father, right? Why would he take photos

of me running through the desert if he was so

adamant he'd let me go when he found me?

Where did those photos go? Harvey was right.

This chaos was only ever going to follow me. I

needed to get out of here. Free the boys of the

burden of having me around. They couldn't be

attached to this. Charlie had started a whole new

life to be free from this. What gave me the right

to drag him back into it and what gave me the

right to get Sebastian involved in it too? I had to

stop ruining people's lives. Otherwise the men I

loved most would end up like Joe. And it'd be because of me.

My body started jolting from side to side but I didn't notice until I heard my name being called. There were two bodies both sides of me, their hands on me. My eyes were open but my vision was now so unfocused I could not make anything out. I could hear their voices but nothing was registering, just the tones of their voices becoming louder and more panicked. It was not until one of the bodies crouched down in front of me and clasped my face in their hands that I gasped for air.

'Kate? Can you hear me?' I started trying to catch my breath as though I'd held it for minutes. Sebastian was kneeling in front of me, his hands were the ones on my face. He pushed my hair out of the way as Charlie rushed back from the kitchen with a glass of water, placing it in front of me.

'Do you want a drink?' I shook my head frantically. He stepped back and placed it down on the table. Sebastian, now holding my hands, was staring back at me. My eyes were desperately searching his face. I was scared.

'I don't want you to die', I whispered, and he frowned at me, his eyes now searching mine, trying to figure out what the hell was going on.

'I'm not going to die Kate. We're safe here, remember?'

'I don't think you are. I don't think either of you are. Not while I'm here.' Charlie stepped forward.

'Katy. What are you talking about? What are you thinking of doing?' A couple of tears fell from my eyes. My gaze was still fixed on Sebastian.

'Harvey. I think Harvey is lying.' Sebastian looked behind to Charlie. I noticed them muttering but could not make anything out. Charlie moved forward and crouched down in front of me, swapping places with Sebastian.

'Listen to me. You are safe here. Even if he is lying, they cannot get to you.'

'I can't rest until I sort this out. We're all acting like this is normal, like I haven't killed someone. Harvey knows it's you and I don't doubt for one second he hasn't told our family. They won't let this lie. There's only one thing that I can do.' They both looked at me with apprehension.

'Katheryn, whatever you're thinking about, think it through properly.' I took a deep breath.

'I'm going back to New York. I'm going to face them all, about everything, and I'm going to do it alone.' Both of the boys were now standing in front of me and without any hesitation they both yelled.

'No!'

Forgetting how weak I felt, I stood up and swayed a little. Sebastian steadied me by putting his arm underneath mine.

'Careful. Kate, is this really a good idea?'

'I need to sort this out by myself. I don't have any right dragging you two through this. Charlie, you have already been through all of this and, on top of all of my fuck ups from the past week, it's best if you stay here and lay low.'

Charlie started pacing again. His hands running through his hair intermittently, Sebastian was still holding on to me.

'So what about me? I've flown all this way to be with you, to look after you, to protect you, and you want to leave and head back? Go

back to the family that cut you off? And you

expect me to let you trust a man that put you in

extreme danger? You want to go and make nice

with *them*? Please tell me you haven't forgotten

what they did to Charlie?' His words were

hushed but sharp, they got my back up slightly

causing me to pull away from his support.

'I know what they did to him and I know

what they've done to me but if I keep running

from them I'll never sleep. I at least have to go

back and admit what I've done is wrong. But, as

soon as they realise that I know everything,

they'll have to let me off the hook. I'll happily

give up my spot in the family, they can kill me

off all they like. You're going to stay here, with Charlie. If you come with me, you'll be at risk.'

'AND YOU WON'T BE? Katheryn this is ridiculous!' Sebastian shouted so loudly it even makes Charlie jumped out of his skin. He stopped in his tracks and turned to look at me.

'You think I never thought about doing that twenty years ago? You think the thought never crossed my mind of going back and trying to bargain with them?' I walked towards Charlie. He was frowning heavily towards the ground.

'I know Charlie, I'm sure you did but you did nothing wrong twenty years ago. It was all on them, they were fucking awful to you. You and Jones. This time round, they have something on me and I have something on them

and they know damn well I will tell the whole

world about what they did if they even threaten

to send me down for murder.' He looked up at

me through his furrowed brow. His face began

to soften before he looked over at Sebastian,

who was now standing with his arms crossed.

'She has a point you know.' I cracked a

small smile

'You are kidding Charlie? You're going

to let her do this?' Sebastian leapt forward and

was now standing in front of us, aggressively

pointing at me.

'*Let* me do this? Sebastian, I'm doing it

whether either of you like it or not. I do not

need your permission!' I strutted off into

Charlie's bedroom, grabbing his laptop from the desk.

'Charlie? This is crazy! Why aren't you stopping her?' All I heard was Sebastian talking at Charlie and not getting any response. I walked back in, laptop in hand and sat back down on the sofa.

'Can I?' Charlie nodded his head and I carried on using his computer. A small smirk was forming on his face.

'What are you doing?' I had never seen Sebastian so panicked. He was like a small child going back and forth trying his best to get involved with absolutely no clue on what's going on. Bless.

'I'm buying a plane ticket to New York. Did you sort my money out?' I stopped typing and looked up at him. He went to say something, I was assuming something more to stop me but he gave up and reached into his back pocket pulling out his wallet. He handed me a new bank card.

'Here. I got us a joint bank account so I could transfer the rest of your money over into this account. I haven't touched it, it's all yours.' I took the card from his hands.

'Thank you.' I copied the details from the card onto the computer, purchasing my plane ticket.

'When are you going?' Charlie's voice softly came into the conversation.

'Tomorrow. One o'clock.' I kept my eyes fixed on Charlie but I knew for certain Sebastian's facial expression was one of disappointment. Thankfully, there was a knock at the door that helped me avoid having to talk about this any further. As much as I knew I needed to go, I hated how this was making him feel.

Charlie put out a selection of Chinese food on the table. He seemed to have ordered for roughly ten people instead of just for the three that were actually there. We all started to tuck in, until Sebastian piped up.

'How long will you be gone for?' He had another helping of rice.

'Only a couple of days at most.' He nodded as he finished his mouthful.

'You're not going to stay in your apartment are you?' I shook my head at him.

'No, I'll stay at a hotel. I'm going to go straight to my parents once I land but I will go back there to tidy and try to get some stuff into storage or something. I'm thinking of putting it up for sale, like you said.'

'You're selling your apartment?' Charlie joined in.

'Yeah, I just don't think it'll be a good idea staying in New York. No matter what will go down tomorrow, I think I've had my time in the city.' He smiled at me and looked at Sebastian.

'You ok with this bud? Don't you have your job and family in New York?'

'I'll get a job anywhere, I'm only a bank manager. My mum and sister will be ok, I've already mentioned it to them and they seem happy for me to move away.' My breath hitched in my throat slightly.

'You've already mentioned it to them?' Sebastian laughed.

'Only a little. I haven't told them everything but I just brushed the idea past them about me and you moving away from the city. They love you. They're happy if I'm happy.' His little confession made me smile from ear to ear, my whole face blushing. I hadn't felt this embarrassed since he kissed me in front of his family last thanksgiving. I had escaped my family meal and made my way downtown. I turned up at Sebastian's family home and his whole extended family were there. He introduced me to every one individually. Later on there was the tradition of taking a family photo. I offered to take the picture but he grabbed me and we stood front and centre surrounded by all of his cousins. The photo was taken, there was cheering, and all of a sudden Sebastian grabbed me and kissed me. Not just a casual kiss on the cheek but a full on lip locking kiss. The cheering continued until we pulled away and I immediately hid my head in his shoulder. As embarrassing as they were, I missed those days.

The sun had set in the Californian sky and there was a bittersweet taste in the air as we tidied away the remains of dinner from the table, putting the leftover food into the fridge. We were almost moving around the kitchen and lounge in harmony. I stopped for a second and saw the boys tidying the lounge, one of them putting the duvet on the sofa, the other pulling the blinds down. In this moment, I didn't want to leave. In this moment, I felt I could stay here forever. Sebastian wandered over to me and kissed me on the forehead.

'I'm going to head to bed in a bit, I'm exhausted.' I held him in an embrace, my ear against his chest. It was nice to feel his chest rising and falling, I felt calm. I took it in just in case I didn't get to feel this for a while again.

'I'll join you. I didn't sleep much last night, I could do with a good night's sleep before tomorrow.' He hugged me a little tighter before I pulled away, walking towards Charlie who'd just come out of his room with clothes in his hands.

'I've changed the sheets in the bedroom so everything's fresh. Make yourself at home but please don't have sex.' I burst out laughing but Charlie's face was deadly serious. I stopped myself from laughing just before he opened his mouth to say more on the matter.

'Charlie, oh my god. We won't! You didn't have to ask!' I lowered my head in embarrassment. Sebastian came over and puts his arm around my shoulders.

'I'm being deadly serious. You need your rest!' He pointed his finger at me.

'Dude, I thought you were cool!' I chuckled as I move past him, picking up my bag and heading into the bedroom. I looked behind me briefly and saw the boys shaking hands.

Charlie's bedroom was just like the rest of his home, minimal and tidy. He had a small built in closet which was just two light grey doors that open into an alcove, showing every single plaid shirt he had hanging up, none of them ironed. I grabbed one off the hanger and slung it onto the bed, closing the closet doors. I started undressing as Sebastian walked in, closing the bedroom door behind him. I turned around, standing in my underwear to see him looking back at me with a puzzled look on his face.

'What's that face for? I know my body is a bit bruised but it's not as painful as it looks, I promise.' He scanned my body with his eyes lingering around my bottom half.

'It's not that, it's just…whose are those?' He pointed at my underwear, making me look down. I start laughing. I completely forgot I had Charlie's boxers on!

'Oh god! They're Charlie's! I had no new underwear and he gave me those this morning!' Sebastian laughed and pulled me closer to him.

'I mean, they do look hot on you.' He tried to lean in for a kiss but I pulled away, making him frown.

'Don't. We're not doing *that*, here.' He let out a playful sigh, pulling me back and kissing me. For a quick second I could've lost myself in that kiss. Sebastian pulled away smiling at me and I turned back to the bed, reaching for the shirt and slipped it on as he began to undress. I crawled into the bed, pulling the covers up. I looked over and Sebastian was crouched over his second smaller bag in just his pants. He unzipped it, picking it up and placing it on the bed.

'Charlie asked me to grab some things for you from the apartment.' I moved across the bed, pulling the bag closer to me. The bag was full of my clothes, and a pair of shoes, as well as a pair of sunglasses and a beanie hat. Sebastian did know we're in California in the middle of August right?

'Thank you! Why the beanie hat?' I pulled it out and placed it on top of everything else.

'I thought at some point you might need a disguise.' Sebastian's face was dead serious. Mine, however, was not. I was trying my best to keep a straight face but my eyes were filling with water from the pressure of not erupting with laughter. The longer he was staring at me with such a serious face the harder it was for me to not laugh, until it got to the point where I gave up and gave in to the hilarity.

'Please tell me you're kidding!' The tears started to fall down my face and Sebastian's face still didn't change, making it all the more funny.

'Don't laugh at me! I'm being deadly serious! I was in a rush and I just thought you might need it!' I wiped my face and calmed myself down as I sat up on my knees reaching up to Sebastian.

'Sorry for laughing. I appreciate it, I really do!' I moved my hands up to his face and ran my fingers through his hair. 'You have to admit, it is a little funny though?'

'Kate.' He looked at me with such naivety in his eyes. We stared at each other until Sebastian began to chuckle. He lowered his head, leaning his forehead onto mine, causing us to both laugh.

'Have I ever told you how much I love you?' He kissed my forehead.

'All the time.' I looked up and kissed him back on the lips. He placed the bag back onto the floor and got under the covers as I moved back to my side of the bed. I laid my head down on the pillow, looking up at the ceiling. Sighing heavily at the thought of having to go back to New York. Am I really ready to face them all? Not one bit. Will I ever be ready? Never.

# CHAPTER THIRTEEN

Six o'clock in the morning, my eyes were wide open with no chance of getting back to sleep. I looked beside me and Sebastian was still fast asleep. I slowly rolled out of the bed, checking my reflection in the small mirror hanging on the wall. As I stood up, the plaid shirt I was wearing drops down, covering me down to my knees. I tip toed across the room, opening the

door into the lounge, trying my hardest not to
wake either one of the boys. The bedroom door
closed softly behind me. I looked over at the
sofa and Charlie's feet were hanging off the
edge, the spare duvet slowly falling off. I
quietly made my way over and gently placed
the duvet back over his body, before heading
over into the kitchen. I turned the kettle on and
it felt like hours pass before it finished boiling. I
poured the water, making myself a cup of tea. I
turned around and Charlie was still sound
asleep.

The sun had only just risen as I unlocked
the front door and headed out into the front
garden. I sat down at the small table and chairs
underneath the oak tree, pulling my knees up to

my chest, clutching the mug of tea. It felt so calm there. The amount of times I'd spent in New York, sitting on the roof of my apartment early in the morning watching the sun come up with a cup of tea and the whole city was already buzzing. There was never any rest for New York but here you could hear the birds, you could hear people starting their cars for the first time that day, you could hear the occasional baby waking up. We may have been twenty minutes from Los Angeles but you would never know it. I looked up into the pale blue sky, not one cloud in sight. I took a sip of my tea and leant my head on the back of the chair closing my eyes. It was nice to hear nothing but birds chirping.

I was able to be alone for ten minutes before I heard the front door open and footsteps walking closer to me. Charlie walked up to the table, already dressed for the day, pulling the second chair out and sitting down, putting his cup of coffee on the table.

'Morning. Did you sleep ok?' I opened my eyes and looked at him, smiling.

'Morning, I did. Though I should be asking you that question, you didn't look too comfortable this morning...' He picked up his coffee, blowing on it before taking a sip.

'It was alright, not the worst I've slept.' He took another sip of his coffee. I didn't know if it was the fact it was early in the morning or something else but Charlie was acting a little off.

'I didn't wake you earlier did I?' He shook his head.

'No, I didn't hear a thing, I usually wake up around this time anyway.' I nodded my head in response. We sat in silence for thirty minutes before I headed back inside, leaving him sitting in the garden.

I went back into the bedroom and Sebastian was still asleep. I closed the bedroom door behind me and crouched down to unzip the small bag with my clothes in. I pulled out a red summer floral tea dress along with a cropped denim jacket and some underwear. I then opened Sebastian's main bag, pulling out his toiletries, all organised in a roll up bag with each item having it's on compartment. Only he would be this organised. Very much the ying to my yang. Sebastian rolled over in bed and it startled me. He reached out his arm over to my side of the bed. Noticing I was not there, he mumbled my name. I placed the things in my hands down on to the side of the bed and walked round.

'Hey, I'm here. I'm just going to get in the shower and I'll be back.' I grabbed his hand to let him know I was there. He opened one eye and smiled at me. 'Go back to sleep, it's super early.' I pulled the covers back over him. Grabbing my clothes and the toiletry bag, I made my way to the bathroom, noticing Charlie was no longer sitting outside. I knocked on the

bathroom door but it just opened as I put my

hand up to it. I looked around back into the

lounge making sure I hadn't just missed him,

but he was definitely not there. I walked over to

the window and his car was no longer parked

outside. Maybe he'd gone to fix his mood.


I don't know about you but shower time

was always a time where I planned and thought

things through, and this one was no different. I

rinsed my hair and I was planning what I was

going to say to my family, trying to psych

myself up to make sure I didn't cry out of anger

when I went to confront them. I stepped out of

the shower and realised that I had managed to

plan all but nothing. No amount of planning

would make this any easier. I met my reflection

in the mirror over the sink. I started gazing at

myself. I looked more recognisable than I did

when I was at the motel. We can thank the sleep

for that but the person looking back at me was

different. She'd evolved, only slightly but still. I

could feel the change in my bones. I could feel

the change in the fact I was not anxious about

going back home. I suppose it was because I

had a safety net this time. I had somewhere to

come back to. I was not scared. No, I was

definitely scared, I would just cry about it later.


There was a knock at the door just as I

was getting into my fresh clothes. I opened the

door and Sebastian was standing there, already dressed and holding my blue velvet makeup bag.

'I packed this in my main bag. Not that you need it but thought it might help you, you know, war paint.' He winked at me, handing over the small bag. I grabbed it from him. I didn't think I'd be so grateful for a man telling me to put on makeup.

'Thank you!' I wrapped him in a hug and walked back over to the sink, starting to now apply my make-up, Sebastian followed me in and sat on the edge of the bath.

'Charlie just came back, he's acting a little weird. Do you know what's up with him?'

I applied my mascara, looking at Sebastian through the mirror.

'I have no idea. He was a bit off this morning, I came in to see you and then went to have a shower and he was gone. Did he say where he went?' Sebastian shrugged.

'No, he didn't say anything. He had a bunch of shopping bags though. I had just come out of the bedroom when he walked through the door. He said 'Hi' and then just went in to the bedroom. He hasn't come out yet.' I turned round to Sebastian.

'Do you think me going back to New York is messing with his head?'

'Maybe? This is a lot for everyone, I can't imagine what this is like for him. He's spent the last twenty years starting a new life and now it's all coming back up again.' I felt agonizingly guilty.

'It was never my intention to make him feel like this. I just, I don't know what I wanted. I didn't want to make things worse at all, I just wanted to find my brother. He seemed to be alright with everything. I shouldn't have assumed!' My eyes started filling with tears as Sebastian stood up, closing the bathroom door he pulled me into a hug.

'The way he is dealing with this is not your fault. He probably was fine about everything, about meeting you and filling you in about everything initially. The dust has settled and it may not be sitting right. We just need to give him time. Are you sure you want to go home alone?' We pulled away from each other so we could see our faces. He wiped under my eyes where my freshly applied mascara had run.

'I have to, Seb. I have to do this on my own terms but I've been thinking. If it all goes wrong and they do end up getting the police involved and have me sent to prison, then I need you to promise me to stay away from my family. Don't try to fight them. Just, you know, visit me occasionally if you can.' Sebastian chuckled quietly and pulled me back into a hug.

'I promise to always visit you.'

'And you promise to stay away from my family, if I'm not around?'

'I'll think about it.' Sarcasm dripped from his words. I pulled away from the embrace, turning and picking up my belongings before opening the bathroom door to leave. Sebastian followed me through to the lounge and we stopped dead in our tracks when we saw Charlie sitting on the sofa with a large suitcase next to him, his head was in his hands.

'Charlie?' He slowly lifted his head up and looks at us. His hands now clasped under his chin, he began to stand and walks so he was now standing in front of me and Sebastian.

'I've been thinking and I've decided to come with you.' I immediately felt the breath hitch in my throat. Thankfully, Sebastian spoke up first, giving me time to find the right words.

'Are you sure Charlie? Is that really a good idea?' Sebastian rested his hand on my shoulder, gripping it slightly as a sign of reassurance.

'I've had twenty years to think about it and I think now it's time. I'm going purely for Kate. I need closure and so does she.'

'What's your plan exactly when you get there? If you go, you'll be putting Kate in more danger than she already is, surely?' Sebastian's hand left my shoulder and he stepped forward, leaving me behind. His whole body language changed as he got closer to Charlie.

'Bud, I'm not going to put her in danger I promise you. I'm going to help her. I'm going to go with her to confront our family and then we'll come back.' Charlie had his hands up, easing Sebastian back. I went and stand in the middle of them, with my back to Sebastian. He tried to say something to me but I ignore him. All of my attention was on Charlie.

'You don't have to do this for me. I can do this by myself.' Charlie held my hands in his.

'I want to do this. Plus, the fact that I'll be back in New York will make them panic more than you saying you know what happened. As soon as someone recognises me, the news will spread like wildfire. They'll have to come clean.' He had a good point. New York was a minefield for keeping secrets, no wonder they sent him away. I turned around to Sebastian. His face was evidently annoyed.

'It will be fine. At least I'm not going alone?' I tried to add a positive to persuade him but I had a feeling he was going to be pissed until we got back safely to LA. Charlie chimed in, trying also to get him on side.

'You obviously can stay here. We'll be back in a couple of days, if that. You can use my car too, make yourself at home.' Sebastian didn't even dignify him with a response, he turned his back on us and slumped down into the sofa. Charlie walked round the other side and picked up a shopping bag from next to his suitcase and placed it on the table. He pulled out three boxes all containing new phones and lined them up next to each other. Sebastian was watching his every move.

'I got us new phones. You needed a new one anyway Kate, you've got a new number obviously but at least you have a proper phone now. I just treated myself while I was there and I got you one too Sebastian. I didn't want you to feel left out...' Charlie picked the phone and handed it over to him. Sebastian left him hanging until I cleared my throat as a way of forcing him to take it. He eventually took it from him and muttered a small 'Thank you'.

'Charlie, thank you. At least you can contact me when I'm back in New York, Seb.

I'll text you as soon as I land. I'll text you every hour if I have to. This *will* be ok, I promise.' I ended up crouching down in front of Sebastian and his face began to soften.

'Alright, just be safe. If you get into any trouble, you call me ok?'

'I promise.' I stood up and walked into the bedroom. I gathered a few things into my brown leather bag including some clothes and some toiletries, making sure my passport was in there too. I removed the money, the gun, and the burner phone and placed them on the bed. I turned to leave the bedroom but notice Charlie's wardrobe was still full of all of his clothes. I picked my bag up and walked back into the lounge.

Both of the boys were sitting on the sofa, setting up their new phones. I put my bag down on the floor next to Charlie's suitcase and lifted it up. Empty.

'Charlie. Why are you taking such a large suitcase with nothing in it?' He looked up at me and rolled his eyes.

'I'm taking this suitcase so you can bring your belongings back. The holdall beside it has my clothes for the trip in it.' I looked to the other side of the suitcase and he was right.

'Sorry.' He smirked at me and diverted his attention right back down to his phone.

'Here.' Charlie passes me the phone. 'I've set yours up ready for the trip, I've given Sebastian your new number and saved ours into your phone.' I hated how nice it felt to have a

normal phone again. To be able to use it without

being scared someone was tracking me. I

checked the time and realised we had to leave

for the airport.

'Thank you! Shall we get going?'

Charlie and Sebastian jumped up from the sofa

slipping their shoes on.

'I'll drive you both, that is if that's ok

Charlie?'

'Of course, bud. I was going to ask

anyway.' Charlie grabbed the keys from the

kitchen and gave them to Sebastian. I picked my

bag up and placed it over my shoulder, picking

up the suitcase at the same time. Charlie came

over and got his holdall and we made our way out and into the car.

The drive to the airport was much the same as yesterday. Quiet, but instead of tension there was anxiety lingering in the air, for all of us. This time I was sitting in the passenger seat next to Sebastian. The fluctuating sounds of the radio seemed to lighten the mood ever so slightly and it wasn't until we were about ten minutes away from the airport that Sebastian placed his hand on my thigh to stop it from bobbing that I realised how nervous I really was.

Sebastian pulls up in the drop of bay and Charlie jumps out, getting the luggage out of the trunk.

'Hey, everything will be fine, Charlie will look after you and don't forget you can call me whenever, ok?' I kw deep down Sebastian didn't want me to do this but him reassuring me despite that made me feel so much better.

'I'll call you as soon as we land. I'm taking the bank card with me but I left my cash on the bed, use that to buy food or whatever.' I felt myself rambling but Charlie knocked on the window stopping me in my tracks. He gestured for me to get out of the car. I leant over and kissed Sebastian before heading out of the car and closing the door. Sebastian wounds the window down and Charlie leant through the window.

'Text me if you need anything, but make yourself at home, we'll see you in a couple of days.' We all said goodbye to each other, until Sebastian drove off. Charlie and I made our way into the airport and straight to the check-in desk. I showed my ticket to the lady behind the desk and she sent the large suitcase down the conveyor belt, making sure I kept my brown leather bag by my side.. Charlie stepped forward, placing his holdall on the belt.

'Is there any chance I can move my seat to be next to my sister?' The lady looked up at us and then back down to the computer, typing incessantly hard on the keyboard before looking back up.

'I'm afraid not. Economy is fully
booked, but there are two seats in business class
that I can upgrade you to? It'll be an extra $400
each though.' Charlie started to decline but I cut
him off immediately, reaching for the bank card
in my bag.

'Of course, that'll be perfect.' I passed
the bank card over the counter and smiled back
at Charlie. He started to shake his head with a
smile on his face. I nudged him to stop.

'Sorry, I forgot you're the rich one
now!' We both laughed as the lady handed back
my card and we head off through security and
into the lounge to wait for our plane out of here.
We sat down in the leather armchairs and I
could hear my phone ring in my bag. I pulled

my phone out of the bag and saw that Sebastian

had texted me to say he was back home. I put

the phone back in my bag and leant back in the

chair closing my eyes. The lounge was quiet

and you could only hear the occasional clink of

glasses but the unfamiliar noise of jeans moving

against leather grabs my attention. I opened my

eyes and saw Charlie fidgeting in his chair.

'Everything ok?' He looked at me a little

startled.

'Yeah, sorry just uncomfortable. And

nervous. And I need to pee.' I smiled at him.

'The restroom is just over there, we've

got about five minutes before we can board the

plane.' Charlie got up and made a beeline for

the restroom. It brought me a little bit of

comfort knowing he was just as nervous as I was though, come to think of it, this must have been killing him. Going back to your home after twenty years of being exiled and confronting the people that did that to you must be fucking hard. I had to admit I'd been in my head a lot about all of this. The way Charlie must have been feeling must be about a hundred times worse than me.

The tannoy called out our flight details, asking us to begin boarding and I realised Charlie wasn't back yet. I picked up my bag and walked over to the men's restroom. Just as I did, Charlie came out. His eyes were a little bloodshot and his hair looked damp. He had his boarding pass and passport in his hands.

'All good?' Charlie's body language was jittery. I know a panic attack when I saw one.

'Yeah, sorry. Shall we?' I reached out and linked my arm with his as we walked towards the gate. His breathing was heavy and I tried my best to reassure him when we got into our seats.

'I know this is taking a toll on you, but you don't have to come to the house with me. You can just stay at the hotel, keep a low profile, whatever.' He strapped on the seatbelt and looked back at me over the lowered seat divider.

'That obvious, huh? Let's just take it one step at a time. I'm going to try and sleep through this flight.' He slid down into his chair.

'Alright, me too but just nudge me if you need me, ok?' Charlie smiled back at me and put the seat divider back up. I got comfortable in my seat and put on the provided headphones. I scrolled through the films as we began to take off. There was no way I could sleep on my way back to New York City.

# CHAPTER FOURTEEN

It was about 4 hours into the flight once my second movie finished that I realised that once we were to touch down in New York City we actually didn't have a hotel to go to. I grab my phone from my bag in the overhead locker and quickly search to book a hotel. Thank God for airline Wi-Fi. The seat divider next to me slowly lowers and I see Charlie's face looking

back at me.

'Good sleep?' I smile at his sleepy face.

'I forgot how comfy these seats were.

Everything ok?' Charlie looks down at my

phone clutched in my hand.

'We don't actually have anywhere to

stay, I was just looking to see if I can book a

hotel.' He rolls his eyes and flings his head back

laughing to himself.

'The one thing! Any luck?' I look back

down at my phone and scroll through a list of

hotels with no vacancies.

'Nope, think it's a bit last minute,

everywhere is booked up.' Charlie leans

forward putting his arm across our seats.

'We could always stay at your apartment? If that's ok with you of course.' I shift in my seat moving my body so I'm sitting face on to Charlie. A wave of unease comes over me as I think about the idea of sleeping in that apartment knowing my Grandfather and potentially other corrupt people have riffled through all of my things. I start to stutter before I'm able to get any words out.

'We can. I just feel a bit weird about sleeping there, knowing *he's* been there and gone through all of my things. It makes me really uncomfortable. Though if it's our only option…'

'It might be our best option, Kate, seeing as we're two hours from landing and nowhere to go. We were going to go back anyway to pack your things. We would only really need to stay one night if, once we land, we go back, pack your things in the suitcase, tidy up, and then the next day go and see the family.' I suppose one night won't hurt.

'Alright. Seeing as it's our only option.' Charlie reached out his arm and ran his thumb over my hand.

'It'll be ok.' I squeezed his hand on mine until we're interrupted by a flight attendant handing out mini bags of pretzels. She left a packet on the tray in front of me and I was immediately distracted.

'Oh! I love these! My favourite part of flying, hands down!' Charlie just laughed at me while I ripped open the small bag and devoured the lot.

An hour and fifteen minutes after I consumed the mini pretzels, we landed in New York. Walking towards baggage claim, I subconsciously linked arms with Charlie again. I think secretly we were both shitting it. We didn't say much until we picked our bags off of the conveyor belt and stood looking at each other, waiting for the other person to say something. We both inhaled and simultaneously said;

'Ready?'

The walk from baggage claim to getting into a taxi and the ride from the airport to my apartment in Brooklyn was a blur until I found myself standing outside my building. The noises of New York city seem louder than before, the smells and the sounds were almost overwhelming. Charlie paid the cab driver and walked up behind me, carrying the suitcase with him. He placed his hand on my shoulder, bringing me back to reality.

'One step at a time.' He moved to stand beside me and held his hand out for me to take. I looked up at him and his eyes read that he's just as anxious to be in New York as I was. We made our way into the lift and headed up to my loft apartment. The doors opened and there was my front door. A pale grey colour but now with added dents from where it was broken into.

We exited the lift and I reached down to unzip my bag, rummaging through to get my keys. I put the key in the lock and opened the door. I was expecting carnage. My belongings scattered across the floor. But no, I walked through my front door and the floor was clear. There were mismatched piles of my things piled on top of the coffee table and on top of the kitchen counter. My bookshelf was no longer organised but the books had been put back, albeit back to front and upside down.

'I thought you said your place had been trashed?' Charlie closed the door behind him as I stand in the middle of the apartment, astounded.

'It had. Sebastian said it had been broken into and that my stuff had been raided.' I was truly astonished.

'Who else has access to your apartment? Obviously apart from Grandpa?' I turned around to look at Charlie, dropping my bag to the floor.

'Just Sebastian. He used the spare key before he came to LA. He came to get some clothes for me and to pick up a pair of his shoes I think.' The penny slowly dropped. I got my phone out and immediately called Sebastian. He picked up after two rings. Before he even had a chance to say hello, I started talking.

'Did you tidy here?'

'Oh hello, I see you made it home safely. Tidy where?' I sighed down the phone.

'Sorry, hello! My apartment. Did you tidy when you were here a few days back?' Sebastian laughed.

'Yeah, I did. I couldn't stand it being so messy. I just made the mess a little more manageable. I didn't know if or when you were ever coming back and I thought you wouldn't want to come back to how it was, so I just tided. You know what I'm like!' I couldn't help but laugh at his admission. He was right. I did know what he was like. He was the tidiest, most organised man I knew.

'Jesus, Sebastian. Thank you though. I appreciate it.'

'What are you doing back there so soon though? I thought you were checking into a hotel as soon as you landed?'

'Yeah, we couldn't get a room anywhere so we're going to stay here tonight. It's only late afternoon so I can do some packing and then we're going to see the family tomorrow. Give us some time to rest and go through everything.' Sebastian sighed through the phone.

'You sure you're ok about staying there? Do you feel safe?' I started pacing round the apartment, looking into the two bedrooms at the back, seeing that nothing'd changed.

'I do, actually. Plus, Charlie is here and it's only for one night. We'll be home in no time.' I walked back into the lounge area and Charlie was sat down on the sofa, giving me a thumbs up to ask if I was ok.

'Alright well, keep me updated, ok?' I smiled back at Charlie as I walked towards him, sitting down in the armchair opposite.

'I will, are you ok?

'I'm fine. I've actually been looking at apartments online. I've been thinking, if I get relocated we could rent a nice apartment right around the corner from your brother. Two bedrooms, there's a gym downstairs, and a swimming pool…' I cut him off.

'You do know, if I sell the Brooklyn apartment you don't have to work and we won't have to rent right? I can just buy us a house?'

The line went silent for a second and all I could hear was Charlie snorting.

'Alright, you can stop bragging now. I don't think I'll ever get used to having a rich girlfriend.' I laughed.

'Good, you shouldn't. Right, I'm starving, we're going to get some food in and get to work here but I'll call you before I go to bed, alright?'

'Alright, be safe and stay in touch. Love you.' Sebastian just melted my heart.

'Love you, bye!' We both ended the call and I slid further down into the armchair. I stared at the pile of stuff on my coffee table, noticing it was an accumulation of all of the things I hid under my bed before I left for

Vegas. I looked over at Charlie and he was staring back at me.

'Is he alright?' I cleared my throat, trying not to draw attention to the items on the coffee table. I had no idea how much Charlie knows about the stuff that went on back in New York once he left.

'Yeah, he's great. Just making sure we're alright.' I stood and reached for the pile of papers in front of me, picking them up and walking them into my bedroom. I got half-way across the lounge when Charlie came up beside me and offered to help.

'Here, let me take some, you've got a lot there!' I dodged away from him slightly causing

me to trip over my own footing and the papers
ended up going everywhere.

'Oh god! Sorry! Charlie don't! Let me!'
We both bent down to start tidying them back
into piles, me more frantically than him. I tried
to scurry all of the papers into my pile but it was
too late.

'Kate what is all of this?' He dropped
down onto his knees, beginning to read each
piece of paper in detail.

'Charlie. It's nothing, honestly, let me
just take it all and put it back.' I reached to
grabbed the piece of paper out of his hand but
he yanked it back, looking at me sternly.

'Katheryn. Tell me the truth.' I sat down on the floor with my legs crossed and exhaled, giving up trying to hide all of this.

'Since I can remember I've always kept the clippings of the articles that would be published whenever Mum and Dad would host a memorial evening for you. They do it every year. It started out as newspaper clippings. There's a piece one of the papers did on the day of your funeral. Eventually, these memorial evenings they would host became some kind of social event and more and more journalists would attend and write pieces on how well our family were coping or the things the family businesses were achieving. Soon enough, it was never about you. So, I just collected everything that *was* about you. It's all I had. Then, when I found out you were alive, the night before I went to Vegas, I got all of this out. I started to try to piece things together and maybe find out why you'd gone and where you were. I didn't get very far but Grandpa came round and saw everything. I think that's why he trashed the place, I don't know. But this is most of it.'

Charlie started picking up more articles and reading them in detail, his breathing getting heavier and before I could say anything to make it better, tears were falling out of his eyes.

'Charlie. I'm so sorry. I'll get rid of it all.' He wiped his face with his sleeve, still reading the articles.

'No. Don't get rid of it.' He finally looked at me and I reach forwarded to hold his hand.

'Are you sure? It's all lies. It doesn't mean anything.'

'That's exactly it. It's also proof. Proof that this family is completely corrupt.' He pulled away from me and moved the papers around, taking out one of the glossy magazine articles that had a full page spread of the fifth anniversary of his death. He pushed it towards me. 'Look. I was dead for five years and they choose to do a photoshoot at home, looking happy and recovered? I'm assuming they got paid for it?' I looked up from the photo in front of me and stared at Charlie. I could feel the guilt

dripping out of my eyes.

'Ten grand. And we got to keep the

clothes.' Charlie sighed and ran his hand over

his face in disbelief. I stared back down at the

article in my lap. I started to trace my fingers

over my eight year old face. I only remembered

parts of that day. Like, the fact my Mother kept

on telling me to smile, to keep my posture

straight, and how the dress they wanted me to

wear resembled something of a tiny meringue

with a sash tied up as a bow. I remembered it

feeling staged. I remembered my Mother

putting on such a façade as soon as the

photographers walked through the door. She

was carrying around a handkerchief in her hand

for the whole three hours they were in our house and every now and then she would dab it under her eyes whenever Charlie's name was mentioned, despite there being no tears for it to soak up. I looked back up and saw Charlie standing above me. Tears dropped from my eyes and he crouched down in front of me.

'I don't blame you. Not one bit. They are the ones in the wrong. You know that don't you?'

'If I just found out sooner, then maybe all of this wouldn't have happened.' Charlie sat down on the floor and wiped the tears off of my face.

'Hey. You can't change what's already happened, neither can I. But, what we can do is make sure we don't do the same again. You

know who told me that?' I shook my head.

'No?'

'You. You told me that and that's

exactly what we're going to do. It's so fucked

up what's happened to both of us and how they

think it's ok to do this but we are going to break

the mould. We're not going to let this continue

anymore. I refuse to stand by and let them keep

lying like this.' I cleared my throat and pushed

my hair behind my ears.

'Ok, but one request?'

'Anything.'

'We do it now. Before one of us loses

our bottle.' Charlie's eyebrows raised and I

raised mine back at him.

'Deal.' My eyes widen. I didn't expect him to agree. We both stood up immediately. Charlie started to sift through the articles on the floor, dividing them into separate piles.

'Do you have a bag or something that we can put these in? We'll take them with us in case we need them.' I ran into my bedroom and found my old tote bag.

'Here.' I chucked it at Charlie from the bedroom door and he caught it with one hand. I went back into my bedroom and lifted up my mattress. The one place my Grandfather didn't check. There they were. My diaries. Not only do they have every secret I've ever had but they also have every piece of information I'd overheard along with the dates and times I heard it. At least I'd managed to gain one thing

from being in this family. Always have

evidence.

# CHAPTER FIFTEEN

Within fifteen minutes of making our decision

to confront our parents tonight, we were in a

cab driving across the Brooklyn bridge. Charlie

was sitting beside me, the tote bag was resting

on his lap, his leg bobbing up and down. Like

brother like sister. I rested my head on the

window and looked out at the passing cars and

the bright lights of the city. I could live in New

York for the rest of my life and never get bored of it.

As we cruised down FDR drive, the sun began to set over the East River. We came to a standstill as we hit traffic going through the United Nations tunnel. I moved my gaze over to Charlie. We both smiled at each other.

'Nervous?' I gestured towards him, now clutching the tote bag.

'Yeah. It's weird. I feel like I'm home but also have this heavy anxiety about being here. I'm getting conflicting emotions.'

'I feel the same. It's like, we should feel safe because we're back home, where we're from, where we grew up, but it feels like our brains won't let us. I get it.' Charlie reached

across and held my hand.

'At least we're together.' I squeezed his

hand in response. Slowly but surely, we made

our way into the city, pulling up outside our

parents building. There was a hustle of people

walking through the lobby so we sat in the car a

little longer until they disappear. Once the coast

was somewhat clear, we both hopped out of taxi

and headed straight inside. We both walked to

the elevator. Pressing the button, I turned to

Charlie.

'How do you want to play this? I can go

in first if you like, scope them out? You can

stand by the elevator until you're ready?' The

elevator doors opened and we both walked inside, waiting for the doors to close.

'No, we'll walk in together. We'll rip this band aid off together.' Charlie leant forward and pressed the button to take us up to the top floor. Home. As the elevator rose and eventually landed at our stop, the sound of music hit us in the face as the doors open. Charlie and I both looked at each other with frowns, just as we stepped out into the foyer. I went to walk around the corner but Charlie put his hand out to stop me. He pushed me back and leant his head around the corner instead.

'They're having some kind of party? There's a massive board with your face on it by the fireplace?' In that moment my heart sinks.

345

They wouldn't have killed me off as well, would they? The elevator dinged and Charlie pulled me into the coat closet, locking the door as he shut it.

'Do you think they've…?' I whispered to Charlie. His brow was fully furrowed now. He held his ear to the door, gesturing me to do the same.

'I don't know, but listen!' I move over and put my ear to the door. All of a sudden I could hear the clinking of wine glasses and then my Mother's voice booming through the apartment via some kind of PA system.

'Thank you all for coming tonight. It means so much to my husband and I that you're all sharing this evening with us. The past week has been devastating for our family, especially

coming off of the back of the anniversary of our

sons' death. The tragic disappearance of our

daughter, Katheryn, has truly rocked us.' I

gasped so hard, I hurt my throat. Charlie rolled

his eyes and tried to console me by rubbing my

arm. 'However in the light of this, as a family

and with your support we have been so grateful

of your donations, your very generous

donations, to the Simmonds Family Trust. This

charity we have set up is to help other families

in need who have lost children. Whether they

have gone missing like our Katheryn, or died

like our beloved Charlie, we hope to be able to

help others who are in need. Thank you again

for coming, please help yourselves to the wine

going around.' A round of applause erupted

from the room and it triggered something in me.

Charlie and I moved away from the door.

'I've had enough of this! She's taking

donations for a charity that they've managed to

set up, what, a week since I've been gone?

They're already profiting off of me not being

here, when they paid me off in the first place!

Fuck that, they paid you off when you were

sixteen and have been profiting ever since!' I

unlocked and opened the door with force,

almost galloping though the foyer to the main

room where the soiree was being held. Charlie

shouted out my name to stop me but instead it

caught the guests' attention, creating a

symphony of gasps throughout the room. I saw

my Mother's face staring at me, her eyes glaring
at me. I walked over to the centre of the room,
grabbing the microphone and standing up on to
the sofa. Clearing my throat, I began to speak,
praying to god I didn't fuck this up.

'Hi everyone. Like my Mother said,
thanks for coming. As you can see I'm not
actually missing. I went away for a bit, didn't I
Mother? Now I must say you put on a
frightfully good party for someone who's
grieving. Now, what are you more sad about
today? The fact that I've been missing and
you've known all along where I've been or the
fact that your son is dead? Oh wait, sorry
everyone, so sorry! Can I just ask a quick
question? Out of everyone here, who's made a

donation to the Simmonds Family Trust?' Every single hand in the room goes up. 'Oh my! That is an awful lot of you! I'm so sorry to say but you've been absolutely defrauded out of your money! Now, now, I can hear you all whispering, what about Charlie? Surely, the money will help people who've actually lost their children. Sadly, you're mistaken. Isn't that right Mother? Grandpa? Father? Have anything to add? No?' I get very cocky when I'm angry but I love it. My Grandfather came sprinting over, trying to pull me down off of the sofa.

'Get down right now, Katheryn. How dare you act like this. You're upsetting your Mother!' I looked over to her and she'd not shed one tear. She wasn't upset, she was terrified because she knew I knew. I brought the microphone back up to my lips.

'She's not upset. Did anyone notice how she didn't greet me? Anyone notice how she hasn't reached out for her missing child? She's heartless. So heartless that she's lied to you for the past twenty years. Charlie isn't dead. He never died, he never got into an accident. In fact, I've been staying with him for the past few days. Charlie?' I turned my attention towards the entrance of the main room and the rest of the room followed my gaze. I was half expecting Charlie to saunter out, scared and frightened, but seemed we were just the same when we get angry. He strode out, past

everyone and joined me up on the sofa. I passed
him the microphone.

'Hi, Mum. Hi, Dad. Grandpa. Hi,
everyone. Sorry to crash the party and put a
downer on the evening, but Kate's right.
They've been lying to you and taking your
money. The money you've donated was never
going to help other suffering families, it was
simply to line their pockets. It's as if they can't
get enough. Oh, and I'm not dead. They just
told everyone that I was just to cover up more
secrets. Isn't that right, Grandpa?' We both
looked down at the three of them standing in
front of us, each of them seething with anger.
Echoes of disbelief filled the room, until an old
familiar voice broke it up.

'It's true. Everything they're both saying, it's true.' Harvey Fernsby steps forward out of the crowd from the bar. Mr and Mrs Simmonds, and Mr Simmonds Senior, paid them off to leave the family. They then paid me to make sure Katheryn disappeared. Twenty years ago, they paid my Father to do the same to Charlie. I have all the evidence you need.' A lump in my throat formed as I saw his face. I was grateful he was for once being honest. I mimed a thank you his way. His words silenced the room into shock.

'I suggest everyone should leave now. I'll personally refund everyone's money. My family and I need to have a little chat.' Every person in the room started to scurry off into the elevator. Charlie and I stepped down off of the sofa. I walked over to the makeshift bar and grabbed two glasses of champagne, before turning to talk to Harvey.

'Why did you do that? Thought you hated me.' He sipped the wine he was already holding in his hand.

'What you said in the hotel room. It really struck a chord with me, and you're completely right. I wanted to be like my Father and I'm not. It's not what I want to do or who I want to be. It's the least I can do.' I was truly surprised I managed to get through to Harvey of all people. I went to walk away with the champagne in my hands but Harvey stopped me.

'I also want to say I'm really sorry about what I did to you. I should never have even thought about the things I did to you. There is no excuse for that kind of behaviour and I give Sebastian my full permission to kill me when he sees me.'

'Thank you for apologising. You want to stay for the fireworks? I might need to ask you for a favour later on.' He nodded as if he knew what I was thinking about. He put his wine glass down and followed me back to the sofa.

The apartment was finally empty of all of the defrauded guests as I sat down on the sofa next to my brother. Harvey sat down in the armchair next to us as I handed the champagne to Charlie. William and Eleanor slowly made their way to the sofa opposite and sat either side of Grandpa. The silence became overwhelming, until someone spoke up.

'I thought I told you to stay away?' Grandpa leant forward aiming his words at Charlie. He simply sipped the champagne and lingered on his response.

'You did, but I'm back now. Think after twenty years we all need to have a little catch up. I see you've tried to kill off another one of your children, and for what exactly? Just money? Or was it ego? Oh wait, it was both! You should try mixing it up next time!' I tried to stifle a laugh but it was no good.

'Look, Charles! We did that for your own good!' Grandpa stood pointing his finger at him. Charlie retaliated but standing too he edged closer. They were almost nose to nose.

'My own good? You did it to cover up my Mother's murder! You've been paying this woman for years because HE couldn't keep it in his pants!' Before Grandpa could react, Eleanor piped up.

'Katheryn, go to your room! You don't need to hear this!' I scoffed. Launching myself off of the sofa, I moved to stand in front of Eleanor.

'Are you fucking kidding me? I know everything! I know that Dad was having affairs, I know Grandpa has been paying you for years just to stay in the marriage, and I know that when my biological Mother fell and hit her head you didn't bother to save her. None of you did. You let her drown and you used Charlie to cover it up. Ever since then, you've been coining in on the fact that you lost a child. But he wasn't yours and neither am I. Look at us now! Nothing has changed, you're still making money off of children that were never yours.' Eleanor stood up and slapped me hard across the face. The force of it knocked me off my footing. Harvey steadied me just before I fell.

'How dare you! I raised you, I put a roof over your head, and to be spoken to like that? You're damn right, you're no child of mine!' I laughed in her face.

'You didn't raise me! We had an abundance of nannies after you killed my

Mother! You didn't come to one of my dance recitals, not one of my Christmas plays. You didn't even realise I moved out until last week, when Grandpa came to my apartment!' I looked at William and he just watched it all unfold. I moved out of Harvey's grip and stood next to Charlie. He checked if I'm ok and we both turned to William. Meanwhile, Harvey walked off into the hallway, using his phone.

'Nothing to say?' Charlie's words stung the air. William hung his head down, still silent. Grandpa looked over at him and shook his head, looking back at Charlie.

'What do you want him to say, Charles? What do you want me to say? Yes, I've been paying Eleanor to stay, yes we paid you both off to leave town, and YES we left your Mother to drown but what are you going to do about it?' Grandpa's shouting was so loud that none of us heard the elevator doors open.

'We'll take that as your confession then?' Three police officers walked into the main room with Harvey following behind. I looked at Harvey with wide eyes and he nodded to confirm he was the one who called them.

'You bitch!' Eleanor cursed at me and I stared back at her, unaffected as Charlie pulled me out of the way of the police officers. Each of them were handcuffed and arrested. One of the police officers walked over to us.

'You two will need to come down to the station tonight to give statements about everything that's happened. Mr Fernsby here

has sent us over evidence the past few days but

if you have anything else, please bring it with

you.' The officer walked off following the other

two taking out William, Eleanor and Grandpa

with them. Harvey walked over to us.

'You've been giving them evidence?'

My voice was quiet, I was in shock at how

quickly everything happened.

'After I saw you two in the desert, I

came back to the city and found the old files

from twenty years ago. Everything is

documented in there: emails; money transfers;

the lot. I admitted to everything I did too. I'm

on bail but if it's proven that they paid me to do

everything and if your statement matches, I'll probably be ok.'

'I'm guessing you didn't mention sexually assaulting my sister?' Yikes Charlie.

'I did. But without Katheryn's statement, they can't charge me.'

'If they even will.' I immediately regretted saying that out loud because, as soon as I did, Charlie had swung round to face me, his voice about ten decibels louder than it should be.

'He sexually assaulted you, Kate, not to mention spiked your drink and caused you to accidentally fire a gun, shooting someone in the back!' He thankfully whispered the last part of that sentence.

'I know Charlie. I was there, remember? But what I'm saying is, even if I do give a matching statement, which I will, it's very unlikely they'll charge him for that. Maybe a few hours of Community Payback. I don't know! I do know that he's apologised to me and I do know that I believe him when he says he's doing the right thing. That's all I can ask for. Being a girl and growing up in a city like this, or any place for that matter, and not to be sexually harassed or abused is rare. You almost get used to it. At the end of the day, you just have to hope and pray that the people that do these god awful things change. That they learn their lesson. That they grow the fuck up and learn to respect women. For the rest of my life, I will have to prove that I am not an object for other people's satisfaction because I am a woman and if that means being face to face with the person that's abused me and accepting their apology and have them know I will make their life hell if I find out that they've done this again, then that's the way it will be.' I took a deep breath and walked away from the boys, picking up Charlie's tote bag from the sofa and my phone from the coffee table. I dialled Sebastian's number and brought the phone to my ear. He picked up after two rings.

'Hey you. How's everything going?' Hearing his voice brought the lump back into my throat. In that second I felt the magnitude of the past hour's events hit me like a tonne of bricks. I scurried down the corridor and into the kitchen.

'There's been a change of plan. We confronted them this evening. They've just been arrested and we have to go and make statements at the station.' My voice was shaky and all the words came out as if it's once sentence.

'What? Are you ok? Is Charlie with you?' I could hear in the background that Sebastian turned the TV off.

'I'm fine, just a bit shaky. Charlie's here, so is Harvey.'

'What the fuck is he doing there?' Sebastian growled down the phone.

'It's alright. He's actually the one that got them arrested. He's been giving evidence to the police since he came back to the city. He's even handed himself in. I just have to give my statement and all of this will be over.' I heard him sigh heavily.

'I swear to god if he goes anywhere near you –'

'I know, you'll kill him. Charlie is with me, he's just as mad as you are but trust me, please?' Just as I finish my sentence, Charlie walked through the kitchen door asking me if I'm ready to go.

'It's not you I have a hard time trusting. Text me once you're back at your apartment safe and sound ok?'

'I will. I love you.'

'I love you too.' I ended the call and left the kitchen walking back into the main room. Harvey was standing by the elevator and Charlie was texting someone on his phone.

'Ok, let's go.' I walked towards the elevator as it opened. Harvey let me go in first.

'How's Sebastian?' Bless him for trying to make small talk.

'Still wants to kill you.' He nodded his head as Charlie walked in the elevator, standing in front of me.

'He's not the only one' I slapped Charlie on the back.

The elevator took seconds to reach the ground floor, thankfully, as I could not cope with the awkward silence any longer. We stepped out and into the lobby and, like

lightening, hundreds of bright lights started

flashing through the glass entrance doors. Press.

Charlie and I instantly turned our backs.

'Fuck. What do we do?' I asked Charlie,

looking helplessly at him. Before he could even

come up with a plan of action long serving

concierge, Mr Wilkins, ran up to us.

'Mr Simmonds, Miss Simmonds, so

good to see you again. Follow my lead. We will

walk out with you. Mr Fernsby, you go first, get

into your car and wait for them. Do not talk to

anyone, just head straight for the car. Mr Banks

will have the car door open ready for you. Ok?'

All three of us nod our heads. Harvey turns and

walks towards the flashing lights with his head

down. 'Ready, kids?' I grab Charlie's hand and hold it as tight as I can. Mr Wilkins nods and we turn around. He quickly comes and stands in front of us, leading us out into the unknown. The fresh air hit me, adding to the disorientation of the flashing camera lights. Somehow, we made it into the back seat of Harvey's car. Mr Wilkins closed the door and Harvey began to drive through the sea of reporters. Eventually, we broke free and I breathed a huge sigh of relief.

'Was that Mr Wilkins?' Charlie asked me in disbelief.

'Yeah, he's been there for years.' Charlie looked at me with a fond smile on his face.

'I can't believe he's still there, he used to help me with my gym bag in the mornings before school.' I smiled at Charlie, realising I was still clutching his hand hard. I let go and apologised.

I turned to look out of the window as we drove through the city but the weight that hit me from walking out of the apartment hadn't gone away. I opened the window slightly but it didn't seem to help. My chest felt like it was collapsing. I closed my eyes to try and focus on my breathing but all I could see in front of me were the faces of my parents. Feeling the leather seats against my skin was flooding my mind with the memory of being in the back of the car with Harvey.

'Stop the car!' I shouted at the top of my lungs.

'I'm just pulling up to the police station now!'

'Kate, are you ok?' Charlie put his hand on my arm and I flinched away from him, cowering further into the side of the car door.

'Please, just stop the car!' As soon as the car came to a stop, I bolted out of the door, taking my phone with me. Luckily, Harvey had pulled up in the station car park. I ran to the far end of the car park and called Sebastian. I crouched down at the side of the building, my arms cradling my knees. I couldn't seem to catch my breath. Sebastian answered but I couldn't get any words out.

'Kate? Katy? Are you there? What's going on?' I gasped for air as if I was drowning. My body began to grow weak from crouching, my legs gave out and I slumped down onto the concrete, my back still against the wall. I shut my eyes tight and tried to focus on Sebastian's voice. I swallowed and took a deep breath.

'There were so many reporters outside. We had to be escorted into Harvey's car and then sitting in the back of his car and the leather on my skin just reminded me of everything and I just really want to come home.' I burst into tears. I really wanted to go home. Home to California, where he was.

'Take a deep breath, you're okay now. Is Charlie with you?' I opened my eyes and

looked across the parking lot and Charlie was
stood against the car next to Harvey, watching
me cry into the phone.

'He's next to the car with Harvey. I told
Harvey to stop the car, I just ran out and called
you. I thought I could do this, but I couldn't,
and now I had to make a statement and go
through everything again. I knew Harvey had
helped us out today but I couldn't be around
him. Not yet, it was too soon. He made me feel
sick. He made me want to tear my skin off. I
just, I couldn't do this Sebastian, I couldn't!' I
subconsciously started scratching at my legs,
the tears blurring my vision. I heard footsteps
coming towards me. It was Charlie running
over.

'Kate, I love you and I'm proud of you. You can absolutely do this. As soon as you're done giving your statement, get on the next flight back here and I'll be ready and waiting to pick you up and take you home ok? I love you so much. You are so strong. Do you think you can walk over to Charlie so I can speak with him?' I wiped my face and looked up at Charlie, who was standing over me.

'He's just come over. Sebastian, I'm so sorry.'

'You have nothing to apologise for. Can I speak to Charlie?'

'Yeah. I love you.' I moved the phone from my ear and passed it up to Charlie. He took it from me and backed away slightly. I put my head on my knees and tried to calm my breathing down further. All I could hear were the occasional 'Yeah', 'Ok', and 'Of course', until he ended the call and walked back over to me. Charlie crouched down and I lifted my head. He was looking at me sympathetically as he handed me my phone. I opened my mouth to apologise but he cut me off just as I did.

'Don't. Was all of this because of Harvey?' He moved to sit crossed legged on the concreate opposite me. My breathing was still a bit hitched from the crying.

'A bit. It's just everything. This has been the worst week of my life.' Charlie nodded his head in agreement.

'I felt exactly the same as you. In fact I feel a bit like that now. Being back here feels so uneasy but that's not my fault and it's not your fault. It's their fault. The people that were meant to look after us, whether they were paid to or not, did a terrible job. They manipulated us and threw money at problems just to make themselves feel better and look where it's got them. You're not going through this alone. You've got me now and I'm not going anywhere.' Charlie's eyes welled up causing me to start crying again. I looked to my right and saw Harvey standing by the car still watching us.

'I know earlier I said all that about letting go and moving on, you know about the whole Harvey thing?'

'Yeah...'

'I don't think I can do that right now. I can't be around him. I don't want him near me, Charlie. I just want to get this statement over and done with and then go home. To California, with you and Sebastian.' Charlie clasps my face, wiping my tears with his thumb.

'I promise as soon as all of this is done tonight, we will go straight back home. Sebastian and I have already spoken about this, Harvey will never come near you again. Are you happy to stay here while I go speak with him? I'll come and get you and we'll walk into the station together.' He starts to stand up, helping me up too.

'Yeah, I'll be ok. I'll message Seb.' Charlie walks back towards Harvey. I unlock my phone and text Sebastian.

*'I've just spoken to Charlie. I'm ok, I'm sorry for scaring you. We're going to give our statements and then come straight back home. I can't stand it here anymore. I love you. I'll text you when I'm out. Xx'*

I look over to where the boys are standing. Within moments, Harvey steps back and gets into his car and drives off. I frown at how easy that was to get him to go away. I walk over to Charlie.

'I told him to leave. He's not going to bother you again.' I hug Charlie as tight as I can.

'Thank you.' We pull away and Charlie holds out his hand to hold.

'Are you ready?'

'As I'll ever be.' I grab hold of his hand and we head into the police station, together.

# CHAPTER SIXTEEN

Charlie and I were both bobbing our legs up and down as we waited for someone to come and get us. Every thought was going through my mind and every time someone walked through the doors I tensed up thinking it was Harvey or my parents. I couldn't bear to see any of their faces again. I looked down at my phone to check the time, only to be greeted by the fact that just 2 minutes had passed since I last

checked. I stuffed my phone into my denim

jacket as someone walked up to us.

They escorted Charlie and I into

individual holding rooms. The walls were

white, the floor were a dusty grey, and the

obligatory double-sided mirror was lined one

side of the wall. I'd been sitting in here at least

twenty minutes before someone entered. A

woman walked into the room. She was wearing

a white shirt tucked into black trousers, pairing

it with a black blazer. Her hair was tied back

neatly. She pulled the chair from under the table

and sat down opposite me. Her smile was kind.

She put down her phone and note pad and

reached forward and placed a Dictaphone in

between us both, turning it on.

'Miss Simmonds, I'm Detective Hart, I

need to take a statement from you about what

has happened over the past week and if you

have any additional information that will help

us in our investigation. Are you ok to proceed?'

I nodded my head, wrapping my arms around

my torso.

'Yes.' Detective Hart cleared her throat.

'Miss Simmonds, in your own words,

please tell us what happened on August 18$^h$.' I

shifted in my chair and tried to think back to

that day. The day before everything changed.

'It was a normal day. I joined my

parents for breakfast in the dining room. Neither

of them were talking to each other, but that's just a normal occurrence. My Mother asked me if I was coming to the event that evening and I made a comment on the fact she called my brother's memorial an event.'

'Does this happen often? In regards to your Mother referring to the memorial as events?'

'Yes. As long as I can remember it's always been more of a social event than a memorial. I was very young when all of this happened but I noticed something was off when I was about eight or nine.'

'The fact that your parents weren't talking to each other, is that normal too?'

'Pretty normal. Dad never really gets a say in anything. It's always my Mother or Grandfather. Now I know why.'

'Ok. Continue.'

'After breakfast I went back to my apartment. Neither of them knew about it at the time but I've lived there for about five years. I go back to my parents' house a couple of times a week but the majority of the time they don't notice that I'm not there.'

'Where is this apartment located?'

'Brooklyn.' Hart starts to write down some details as I'm talking.

'Did anyone else know about you living there?' She looked up at me.

'Just my boyfriend.'

'What's his name?'

'Sebastian. Sebastian Delaney.' She scribbled his name down on the pad in front of her.

'Is he in New York at the moment?' Her phone vibrated on the table. She checked it briefly whilst I continued talking.

'No, he's in Los Angeles. He's at Charlie's house. He came out to visit me whilst I was staying with Charlie.' Hart's eyes were still fixated on the phone. She looked up at me and raised her eyebrows.

'Right…going back to the night of the memorial. That's when you overheard your Grandfather talking to your Mother about Charlie being alive, is that right?'

'Yes, that's right.'

'What did you do as soon as you heard that, Miss Simmonds?' Hart's tone was patronising and harsh. Her kind attitude had suddenly changed.

'I left the house immediately and went back to my apartment.'

'Why did you leave?' I frowned at her question, isn't that obvious?

'I left because I was in shock. I'd just found out that my brother was alive and that they'd paid him off to leave. I didn't know what to do, I just knew I didn't want to be there anymore.'

'Did you tell anyone as soon as you found out? Call the authorities?' Her questioning as getting my back up.

'No. I went straight back to my apartment, I didn't call anyone. I stayed up and went through all the paper clippings I had to see if I could figure out if I could find him.' Without missing a beat, Detective Hart jumped in.

'And did you? Did you figure out how to find him?'

'No. My Grandfather came round a few hours later and threatened me. He told me to leave within twenty four hours. He set me up with a private detective and-' She cut me off.

'So he helped you.' I sat up in my chair.

'No. He *set me up*. The private detective who he set me up with was in on it. He told me there was a lead in Vegas, but there wasn't. It was just a ploy to get me out of the way!'

'But you still went to Vegas, knowing the lead wasn't reliable?'

'I went to Vegas, yes, but I didn't know I had been set up or that the lead was fake. I only found out once Harvey told me in the hotel room.' Detective Hart was staring at me intensely.

'Harvey Fernsby, is that right?'

'Yes.'

As soon as I answered there was a knock at the door. A man came in and gestured for Hart to go outside.

'I'll be back in a second.' Turning the Dictaphone off, she left the room, taking her phone with her, her heels clicking down the hallway outside.

I leant back in my chair and exhale. I didn't think I would be interrogated. I was only here to give my statement, to tell them the hell I've been through. I keep thinking about Charlie. I wondered if he was out yet. I wondered if he was having such a hard time. I heard commotion going on outside my room. Hushed voices frantically talking back at each other, when suddenly I heard Charlie shouting.

'Let me see her! Please! Let me just go in and see her!' I instantly stood up from my chair and went to open the door. I tries to turn the handle but it didn't open. I started banging on the door.

'What's going on? Charlie? I can't get out!' I kept trying the handle on the door but it was locked.

'Kate? Can you hear me?' Charlie shouted through the door.

'Charlie? What's going on?' The commotion continued outside the door. I couldn't make out what was happening.

'Kate, I'm going to get you help. I'm going to get you out of here, ok? Don't say anything. Promise me?' The distress in Charlie's voice panicked me.

'Charlie, please tell me what's happening!' I banged on the door again.

'Katheryn. Promise me. Don't say a word until I get you help.' His words were stern.

'I promise.' Charlie moved away from the door and all of the commotion stopped. My mind was racing and I felt physically sick. I started pacing around the room, my eyes filling with tears. I heard the door being unlocked and I turned immediately, facing the two people walking in. Detective Hart re-entered along with a male officer. They both sat down at the table, waiting for me to join them. I didn't. I carried on standing in the corner of the room, staring them out. Detective Hart turned the Dictaphone back on, she gestured for me to sit back down but I ignored her offer.

'Miss Simmonds. Please tell us who Joe Coyne is.'

CPSIA information can be obtained
at www.ICGtesting.com
Printed in the USA
BVHW071008180121
598050BV00009B/167